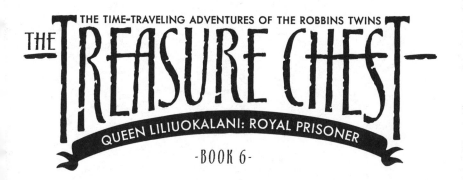

THE TIME-TRAVELING ADVENTURES OF THE ROBBINS TWINS

THE TREASURE CHEST

QUEEN LILIUOKALANI: ROYAL PRISONER

-BOOK 6-

BY *NEW YORK TIMES* BEST-SELLING AUTHOR

ANN HOOD

Grosset & Dunlap
An Imprint of Penguin Group (USA) Inc.

For Cousin Gina

GROSSET & DUNLAP
Published by the Penguin Group
Penguin Group (USA) Inc., 375 Hudson Street, New York, New York 10014, USA
Penguin Group (Canada), 90 Eglinton Avenue East, Suite 700, Toronto, Ontario M4P 2Y3, Canada
(a division of Pearson Penguin Canada Inc.)
Penguin Books Ltd, 80 Strand, London WC2R 0RL, England
Penguin Ireland, 25 St Stephen's Green, Dublin 2, Ireland
(a division of Penguin Books Ltd)
Penguin Group (Australia), 707 Collins Street, Melbourne, Victoria 3008, Australia
(a division of Pearson Australia Group Pty Ltd)
Penguin Books India Pvt Ltd, 11 Community Centre, Panchsheel Park, New Delhi—110 017, India
Penguin Group (NZ), 67 Apollo Drive, Rosedale, Auckland 0632, New Zealand
(a division of Pearson New Zealand Ltd)
Penguin Books (South Africa), Rosebank Office Park, 181 Jan Smuts Avenue, Parktown North 2193, South Africa
Penguin China, B7 Jiaming Center, 27 East Third Ring Road North, Chaoyang District, Beijing 100020, China

Penguin Books Ltd, Registered Offices: 80 Strand, London WC2R 0RL, England

Text © 2013 by Ann Hood. Illustrations © 2013 by Penguin Group (USA) Inc. Published by Grosset & Dunlap, a division of Penguin Young Readers Group, 345 Hudson Street, New York, New York 10014. GROSSET & DUNLAP is a trademark of Penguin Group (USA) Inc. Printed in the U.S.A.

Library of Congress Cataloging-in-Publication Data is available.

Illustrations by Denis Zilbur. Map illustration by Giuseppe Castellano.
Design by Giuseppe Castellano.

ISBN 978-0-448-45729-1 (pbk)   10 9 8 7 6 5 4 3 2 1
ISBN 978-0-448-45739-0 (hc)   10 9 8 7 6 5 4 3 2 1

ALWAYS LEARNING   **PEARSON**

CHAPTER 1

Great-Uncle Thorne Reveals Secrets

Just when Maisie and Felix Robbins thought nothing exciting would ever happen to them again, something exciting happened.

The week of school vacation promised to be muddy (thanks to a steady spring rain) and dull (thanks to Great-Uncle Thorne, who had sealed The Treasure Chest with something impenetrable, or so Maisie believed, since she had tried everything she could think of to get inside).

"Remember when life was thrilling?" Maisie asked Felix with a long, dramatic sigh.

They were sitting in the Library considering their fate: a week with no school, no Treasure Chest, and no mother. Technically, of course, they did have a mother. But with all her time split between work and her boyfriend, Bruce Fishbaum, it didn't feel like they had a mother.

"We're practically orphans," Maisie continued.

"Worse than orphans," Felix said with his own sigh. "In books, orphans have fascinating lives. Our lives are dull as dirt."

Recently, Felix had fallen in love with similes, comparisons using *like* or *as*. *Busy as a bee. Dumb as a post. Happy as a clam.* Usually they drove Maisie crazy, but today the two of them were exactly on the same side: bored.

Maisie rolled a marble around on the special hammered-brass table that their great-great-grandfather had brought back from Morocco a million years ago. She'd found the marble under Felix's bed that morning when she was looking for her lost sneaker. It was blue and milky white and covered in dust. *Maybe it will change our luck,* Maisie had thought. *Like a talisman or good luck charm.*

"Why do you suppose this marble was under your bed?" she asked Felix now.

Felix shrugged.

"Maybe it belonged to Samuel," she said

hopefully, pronouncing the duke's name *Sahm-well*, the way Great-Uncle Thorne said it.

Felix's room was called Samuel Dormitorio, named after a Spanish duke who had stayed there for almost three years back when Great-Uncle Thorne and Great-Aunt Maisie were kids. In those days, all sorts of royalty and rich people came to Elm Medona for visits that seemed to never end. Maisie's room was named after a princess who'd done just that. Princess Annabelle had left her country of Nanuh when her father, the king, was kicked out, and hid at Elm Medona until it was safe for her to go home. No one came to Elm Medona anymore. Unless you counted Great-Uncle Thorne's ancient girlfriend, Penelope Merriweather.

"Maybe it's magical," Maisie said, holding the marble up to the light.

That was when the phone rang. The phones in Elm Medona were all old-fashioned. Some of them looked like boxes and were attached to the wall. They had a big dial in the middle and a funny earpiece that hung from a cord. Whenever Maisie talked on one of those phones, she shouted. She didn't need to shout; the phones worked just fine.

But something about them made her feel that she had to shout to be heard.

Which was why, when she answered this particular call, she shouted, "Hello!"

Her father's laugh came through the phone. "Hello!" he shouted back.

The sound of her father's voice always made Maisie feel happy and sad at the same time. He lived practically across the world in Qatar, where he worked for a museum, and she and Felix hadn't seen him since Christmas.

"Oh, Dad! Life here is so dull!" Maisie shouted.

"Sweetie?" her father said. "Why are we shouting?"

"Oh, it's this silly old-timey telephone, that's all."

"Ah," he said. "Well, I can hear you just fine."

Felix had come to stand beside Maisie as soon as he heard their father was on the phone. He kept motioning for Maisie to give him the earpiece so he could hear, too. But Maisie didn't.

"Guess what?" their father asked.

"You're here in Newport?" Maisie guessed, even though she knew how ridiculous that was. Still, it always startled her how her father could be so far away and yet sound like he was nearby.

"Close," he said, surprising her.

"Close?" she repeated, just to be sure she'd heard him correctly.

"He's here?" Felix said, hopping around in excitement at the idea that their father was in Newport at that very minute.

But Maisie shook her head at Felix.

"I'm in New York," her father said into Maisie's ear.

His voice, those most wonderful words—*I'm in New York*—sounded more wonderful than anything Maisie had ever heard.

"New York?" she said, again just to be sure.

"I am standing on West Eighty-Sixth Street even as we speak," he said.

Maisie looked at Felix. "He's on West Eighty-Sixth Street," she said.

Felix broke into a huge grin.

"And Monday you and Felix are getting on the train and coming here," her father said.

"And *we're* going to New York on Monday!" Maisie said to Felix, shouting again.

"Wahoo!" Felix said.

Wahoo was something his friend Jim Duncan always said, and ordinarily Maisie did not like it. But somehow it seemed perfect right now.

"What did Felix say?" her father was asking her.

"Wahoo!" Maisie said.

That fast, their boring vacation had turned into something marvelous.

Great-Uncle Thorne caught Maisie staring wistfully at the hidden door that led to The Treasure Chest, its seams sealed tight.

"Really," he said, "staring isn't going to make it open."

Maisie turned a steely gaze on Great-Uncle Thorne. "You're mean," she said.

"No, I'm not," he said indignantly. "Selfish, maybe. But not mean."

They stared at each other for what seemed like a very long time.

"Soon," Great-Uncle Thorne said softly, "I will be as frail as Penelope. We will sit side by side, staring out at the sea in a fog of old-age bliss."

"Fine," Maisie told him. "Waste away. I don't care."

She knew that was exactly what would happen if

she and Felix couldn't time travel. Every time they did, Great-Uncle Thorne got healthier and stronger. Who would choose to shrivel up and die, just for love? Love was way too complicated, Maisie decided.

She began to walk back down the hall, but when Great-Uncle Thorne started talking, she paused.

"Besides," he said—and now he was gazing at the sealed-up door—"you two knuckleheads don't even use the power right."

"What do you mean?"

He waved his hands in the air, exasperated. "I mean, you're not purposeful. You just grab objects all willy-nilly and stumble around."

"I tried to let the plans for the Holland Tunnel take us to New York, but Felix—" Maisie began.

"Have you even *used* the anagram?" Great-Uncle Thorne said, ignoring her as usual.

"Elm Medona?" Maisie asked, suddenly interested.

"The *anagram!*" he bellowed.

"Oh, you mean *lame*—"

"Silence!" Great-Uncle Thorne said, lifting his jade-tipped walking stick.

"Uh," Maisie said. "No."

"What do you do, then, when you're in a pickle?"

She looked at him, confused.

"A tight spot?" he added. "Danger?"

Maisie thought of the ship fire and the attack on the village in the Great Plains and fleeing to Shanghai.

"We wait," she said weakly. "I mean, nothing's going to happen to us—"

At this, Great-Uncle Thorne threw his head back and laughed. *Like a hyena,* Maisie thought, even though she disliked similes.

"You two ignoramuses actually think you're invincible?" he said, wiping his eyes. "Because you're not."

"We aren't?" Maisie said, and she actually shuddered, remembering how certain she had been that no matter what happened in the past, they would be safe.

"The anagram can do two things," Great-Uncle Thorne said, holding up two fingers. "One, it can give you necessary information about the person you meet." He folded one finger. "And two, it can get you out of danger." He folded the second finger, and sighed. "Of course, if you *overuse* it . . ." He smiled at her, showing his big teeth. "Well, that doesn't really matter, since you are finished with The Treasure Chest."

"How do you overuse it?" Maisie asked.

"Irrelevant!" he announced, and continued on his way.

Maisie watched him. His gait was already slower. He kind of shuffled now.

"You probably don't know about the shard, either," Great-Uncle Thorne said over his shoulder almost gleefully. "No matter. No matter."

Instinctively, Maisie's hand went into her pocket, where she kept the shard from the Ming vase. She rubbed it between her fingers, as if it might reveal its secrets to her.

On Sunday night, Bruce Fishbaum came for dinner. Their mother had worried all day about what to make, and finally settled on pot roast, of all things. Maisie wasn't sure, but she believed that if a person truly loved another person, she would make something fancy, like duck à l'orange or baked Alaska. She took the pot roast as a good sign of her mother's feelings toward Bruce Fishbaum.

Great-Uncle Thorne and Penelope Merriweather

were eating out that night, which Maisie was grateful for. She did not enjoy watching two people as old as they were making eyes at each other and calling each other pet names like Duckie and Pumpkin.

"Isn't this cozy?" her mother said, standing back to admire the table, set for four with the Pickworth china and the Pickworth silver and the Pickworth crystal. The gardener had brought in pots of hyacinths, and they stood in a line down the middle of the enormous table, sending out their too-sweet hyacinth scent.

"If you consider a table that seats twenty cozy," Maisie said, "then yes, this is quite cozy."

Her mother ignored her. "We'll have appetizers in the Library, then come in here for dinner. And I was thinking that for fun we'd have dessert in the Cigar Room."

"We can't hang around all night," Maisie said. "We need to pack for our trip to see Dad tomorrow."

Her mother was fussing with the hyacinths, straightening each stem and rearranging the colors, moving the white and the pink hyacinths, then the pink and the purple.

"You two are being such good sports," she said.

"Well," Maisie said, "if we want to be fed, we have to put up with Bruce Fishbaum."

"Yes, of course," her mother murmured. "I mean, about Bruce, of course. But about Agatha, too. It shows how well you're adjusting. And I know how hard this has all been—believe me, I know. But I'm so proud of you both."

Apparently satisfied with the hyacinths, she looked at Maisie and smiled.

"Agatha?" Maisie said.

"Oh, dear," her mother said. "Is it Agnes?"

"What are you talking about?" Maisie asked her.

"Your father's girlfriend, of course. Agatha. Agnes. I promised myself I would remember it, but who in the world is named Agatha or Agnes anymore?"

If her mother noticed the look of anger that was spreading across Maisie's face, she didn't say anything about it. Instead, she cocked her head and said, "I hear the doorbell. That must be Bruce." Then she scurried away, leaving Maisie alone in that overly sweet-smelling room.

Felix thought it was very strange that his mother

had made his father's favorite appetizer for Bruce Fishbaum: artichoke-heart mayonnaise Parmesan-cheese chopped-chilies cheddar-cheese dip. His father made that dip every time they had guests over, and now his mother had made it for Bruce Fishbaum.

"What's in this?" Bruce Fishbaum practically moaned.

"My secret," Felix's mother said. Which was what his father always said when someone asked him that question, because apparently adults did not like to eat gobs of mayonnaise.

"Mayonnaise," Felix said to Bruce Fishbaum. He could feel his mother glaring at him.

"No wonder it's so good," Bruce said, unfazed.

Bruce Fishbaum had on a nautical tie, as usual. This one was green, and looked like it had architectural drawings on it, all lines and squiggles and numbers.

"You ever play hockey?" Bruce asked Felix between bites of dip on slices of French bread.

Felix shook his head. "I'm class president," he said.

Bruce pointed at him. "You need to get out on the ice," he said.

"Well," Felix said, "I ice-skate."

Technically, that was true. He had ice-skated in his life, though not for some time. In fact, the last time he had ice-skated was in Central Park with his father and Maisie, the winter before the divorce.

"I like ice-skating," Felix added. Technically, that was true, too. Even though he could think of dozens of things he'd rather do, ice-skating was okay.

"I'll take you sometime," Bruce said. "Show you how to hit some pucks."

"Uh-huh," Felix said, just to be polite.

"Where in the world is your sister?" his mother asked, getting to her feet and looking around, as if Maisie was hiding somewhere in the Library.

"Packing?" Felix offered.

"She was supposed to pack *after* dinner," his mother said.

Bruce Fishbaum waved his hand dismissively. "Relax," he said. "More artichoke-mayonnaise dip for me."

Then he did something that made Felix practically run out of the room. Bruce Fishbaum took Felix's mother by the waist and pulled her down onto his lap.

"Oh," Felix said. He was the one standing now,

looking for an exit. "Um . . . I'll go find her."

As quickly as he could, he got out of that room, and bumped right into Maisie in the foyer.

"Mom is sitting on Bruce Fishbaum's lap," he blurted.

"Dad is in New York with his girlfriend," Maisie blurted back.

Maisie and Felix stood staring at each other. They both understood just how dreadful these facts were.

"Her name," Maisie said, "is Agatha."

"No one's name is Agatha," Felix said.

"Or maybe Agnes."

"That's even worse," Felix said.

Maisie took Felix's hand.

Although neither of them said anything, each knew what the other was thinking. Just a year ago, they were living happily at 10 Bethune Street with their parents. Every day, their father went off on his bicycle to his studio downtown in Tribeca. Their mother studied for the bar exam. Maisie and Felix happily walked to school together, unaware that in just a short time, nothing would be the same. They stopped at the Bleecker Street playground on their way home, and sometimes their father found them there and the three of them walked the rest of the way together. Didn't their mother always look happy when they walked in the door, peering at them over her funny half-glasses that she wore for reading? Didn't their father always kiss her right on the lips? And didn't they sing together while they made dinner, their father slightly off-key, their mother in her beautiful musical theater voice? How had they gotten from there to here, with a Bruce Fishbaum and an Agatha or Agnes?

Their mother and Bruce appeared, both of them smiley and flushed.

Maybe you did make pot roast for someone you love, Maisie thought in horror.

"Do you know what my specialty is?" Bruce asked.

For some reason, Felix felt like Bruce was asking him, so he answered no.

"Fried turkey," Bruce said proudly.

"Ew!" Maisie said, at the exact same time that her mother said, "I've heard that is the way to make a bird. It comes out surprisingly moist, right?"

"Right," Bruce said. "The trick is dropping it in without splashing boiling oil and starting a fire."

"That would be bad," Felix said.

"Mom always puts the turkey in too late, and we end up eating hours after we'd planned," Maisie said. Her chest was constricting, the way it did when she felt saddest.

"That's not true," her mother said, chuckling. "Well, maybe once or twice."

"Tell you what," Bruce said as they all moved toward the Dining Room. "When my kids are home, I'll fry a bird and have all of you over."

"That would be great," their mother gushed. "Doesn't that sound great, kids?"

It was a rhetorical question, Maisie knew. But still she said, "*Fried* turkey?"

Bruce Fishbaum pointed at her. He was a pointer, Felix realized.

"Just you wait," Bruce said.

Neither Maisie nor Felix liked the way Bruce Fishbaum sat at the head of the table, as if he belonged there. They did not like the way he carved the pot roast, or served their mother and then them. They did not like how he poured wine into the Pickworth crystal, or held up his glass and said, "To the beautiful cook." Nor did they like the way their mother blushed and cast her eyes down when he said it.

Somehow, they ate their pot roast and followed their mother and Bruce Fishbaum into the Cigar Room for chocolate pudding.

Finally, the time came when they could excuse themselves, and they did, eagerly. But all of the excitement of their trip had vanished. Maisie went into her room, and Felix went into his, and they each packed their suitcase halfheartedly. Their vacation would begin tomorrow. But instead of going home to New York City and spending the week with their father doing all the things they would have been doing if their parents hadn't gotten divorced, Maisie and Felix were going to be with a woman named Agatha. Or Agnes.

Just before Maisie climbed into her very high bed, she opened her closet door and reached into the trunk that had all the possible anagrams for Elm Medona written on its lining. She took out a small crown she'd hidden there. It glistened with what looked like real jewels, and Maisie ran her hand over them.

Then, she placed the crown on her head and

slowly—regally, she thought—walked over to the mirror. *Ha!* she thought. Great-Uncle Thorne had said they weren't purposeful when they chose the objects in The Treasure Chest. But Maisie had seen the crown and known that it would take them somewhere far away, where kings and queens ruled. Maybe there would be jousting and knights in shining armor. Staring at her reflection, she curtsied.

"Your Highness," she said in a solemn voice.

Maisie kept the crown on for a while longer, parading around her room and waving her hand in the funny half-swivel she'd seen Queen Elizabeth make. Finally, she took it off and put it inside her suitcase. *But wait,* she thought. The crown was bigger than most of the items they'd used before. Maisie retrieved her Mets fleece jacket. No, the crown wouldn't fit in the pocket. Then she remembered that the fleece had an inside pocket that was deep enough to hold her catcher's mitt when she played baseball. True, it left a bulge there, but so what? She tried, and sure enough, the crown fit. Satisfied, she got into bed and promptly fell asleep.

CHAPTER 2

Back to Bethune Street

Maisie and Felix emerged from their train into Penn Station with a good amount of trepidation. Before they knew about this mysterious Agatha/ Agnes woman, the idea of traveling alone by train for three hours and then arriving back in New York City had them positively excited, even though they had time traveled, the two of them tumbling through time and space, always in the exact same way: beginning with the smell of gunpowder and with their favorite smells in the air—cinnamon and Christmas trees and flowers in summer—and the wind whipping around them, then that nanosecond where absolutely nothing happened. They'd landed in a barn, the ocean, a busy marketplace in China, and a roller coaster in Coney Island—even in the midst of a herd of buffalo. There was always the figuring out of where exactly they were, and *when* exactly it was. And then finding the right person to give the object to. Surely nothing was more exciting than that.

Except, once they returned home, it always felt like they had dreamed it. Life went right back to normal. They went to school or ate dinner. Their mother asked them what they were up to, but they couldn't tell her. No time had passed in the present. Not even a second. Even though they'd stowed away on a ship or gone on a dream quest, even though they'd had real adventures, as soon as they got home, everything was as ordinary as ever. So, in the oddest way, traveling solo on a train from the tiny station in Kingston, Rhode Island, to Penn Station in New York City felt even more adventurous than time travel.

Maisie had imagined going to the dining car and eating food that she could only get on a train trip. Although she had no idea what that might be, she imagined it came in a tray with special compartments, each one holding its own course. She imagined sitting at a table with a white tablecloth, and watching

Connecticut roll past. But instead, adding to her overall disappointment, the dining car smelled like microwaved plastic, and the food was completely dull.

And Felix imagined that the trip would be so special it would inspire him to write poetry or something. Jim Duncan had given him a book called *Moby-Dick* to take on the trip, and Felix did try to read it. But the story, about a guy on a whaling ship a long time ago, did not capture his interest. Neither did the journal he'd brought along. Really, all he could think about was his father and Agatha/Agnes. He felt miserable.

By the time they stepped off the escalator at Penn Station and moved toward the big departure board their father had told them to find, the excitement of the week ahead had almost vanished completely.

But then they saw their father standing right where he said he would be, under the big departure board. Alone. He had on his faded jeans and a plaid shirt and the biggest grin ever. As soon as he spotted Maisie and Felix, he ran toward them and swooped them both up at once into his strong arms.

"Is it possible you two are even bigger than at Christmas?" he said into their hair, because he was holding them so tight and so close, that's where his mouth settled.

"I grew half an inch," Felix said proudly. He was tired of being shorter than his sister, even though his mother always told him that boys have their growth spurts later than girls.

"At least half an inch," his father said.

He released them, kind of. He kept one hand on each of them at the shoulder and studied them at arm's length.

"Boy," he said, "have I missed you guys."

For a moment they stood like that. Then, he let them go and took their overnight bags from them, motioning for Maisie and Felix to follow him.

Maisie glanced at Felix.

He shrugged, happily.

Obviously there was no Agatha/Agnes. It was just them and their father. Relieved, they descended into the subway, where they sat, smiling, on the uptown 1 train, their father peppering them with questions the whole way.

"Ta-da," their father said as he opened the door to a brownstone on West Eighty-Sixth Street.

He unlocked the door to one of the ground-floor apartments. Sunlight streamed in from the bay window, spilling a dappled pattern onto the polished wooden floor.

"What is this place?" Maisie asked, stepping inside.

"A friend in Doha is letting me use it," her father said.

He tossed the keys into a big brown-and-orange bowl as if he'd been tossing his keys there forever.

They stood in a small living room decorated in a kind of shabby-chic style, with big, worn easy chairs and a couch covered with pillows. The kitchen was small, too, and there was an alcove with a round wooden table and four chairs, each one painted a different bright color. In the middle of the table sat a big blue bowl, kind of like the bowl that held the keys, full of shiny apples.

"You guys can take the bedroom," their father said, heading in that direction with their bags. "And I'll crash on the couch."

When he disappeared into the bedroom, Felix said, "Not bad, huh, Maisie?"

"Not bad at all," Maisie admitted.

Their father came back out and took a menu

from a corkboard on the kitchen wall.

"Chinese food?" he said, holding it up.

Felix sighed. It sure was good to be back in New York City, where Chinese food could be delivered anytime, anywhere.

"Sounds good," he said.

"I trust you still like dan dan noodles," their father said, scanning the menu. "Kung pao chicken, fried pork dumplings—"

"The usual!" Maisie said.

Their father closed the menu. "The usual," he said, and his voice sounded as happy as Maisie and Felix felt.

For three days, life was almost perfect. Or as perfect as it could be without their mother with them, too. Maisie and Felix and their father walked over to Central Park and played Frisbee. They went to the zoo there like they used to when Maisie and Felix were little. They spent one whole afternoon at the movies, leaving one theater when a movie ended and buying a ticket right away to a movie at another theater. They ate cheap Indian food. They sat around the cozy living room in their pajamas and just talked to each other—about school and life in Newport and their father's job at the museum in Doha, Qatar. He told them about the desert where the sand was said to sing, and a trip he took to Dubai.

But on the fourth day, their father sat at the kitchen table with a big mug of coffee and a look on his face that let Maisie and Felix know that something was up. And that something, they both surmised, had to do with Agatha/Agnes. Maisie studied the mug, which was green and blue and in the same style as all the bowls.

"So," their father said, "remember I said this apartment belongs to a friend of mine?"

"Uh-huh," Maisie said suspiciously.

"And remember a while ago I told you that I was . . . um . . . seeing someone?" he continued.

"You said spring was in the air," Maisie reminded him.

"Exactly," he said. "Well, her name is Agatha . . ."

Maisie and Felix snuck a peek at each other.

". . . and actually this is her apartment. And actually, she's arriving in New York tomorrow."

Maisie and Felix waited.

"You're really going to like her," their father said finally.

They didn't say anything.

"I know this is . . . awkward," he said. "Your mother with Barry—"

"Bruce," Felix corrected him, thinking how neither of his parents could get the name of the other's new partner right.

"I wish it were different," their father said, in a way that made Maisie and Felix believe he did wish it were different.

"Then do something about it!" Maisie said. "It's not too late. I bet people get divorced and marry each other again all the time."

"They probably do," their father said, nodding. "But your mother does not want to marry me again."

His voice sounded so sad that Maisie grabbed hold of his hand. She liked her father's calloused hands, big and rough.

"But," he said, "we got you two out of the deal. How lucky were we, huh?"

They went through the day together doing the things they liked to do, but something had gone out of Maisie and Felix's mood. The next morning, they announced that they wanted to go off on their own for a while.

"A walk down memory lane?" their father said, in that wistful voice he used whenever he talked about the time before the divorce.

Agatha was due to arrive that afternoon.

"Be back for dinner, right?" their father said.

Apparently Agatha was one of the greatest cooks ever, and she was making them all dinner tonight. She'd made all of those bowls and mugs and even the plates because apparently she was also a great ceramist. In fact, Agatha seemed to be great at just about everything. She'd made the quilts on the beds. She'd knitted the scarves and hats and gloves that hung on the hooks by the door. She'd painted the bathroom walls with quotes by her favorite writers.

"Of course," Felix said with forced cheerfulness.

Their father kissed the tops of their heads, made sure they had the key to get back into the apartment, and told them to have a great day.

Without having to discuss their plans, Maisie and Felix walked to the subway, got on a downtown C train to Fourteenth Street, and walked six blocks down Eighth Avenue to Hudson Street. At Bethune Street, they passed by the diner and walked the short block to number 10, where they stood hand in hand, staring at the nondescript front door. They had walked in and out of that front door millions of times, never giving it a second thought. But standing there that day, the plain black door looked almost beautiful.

It opened, and out came Mrs. Morimoro, who had lived next door to them in 1B.

She always seemed angry, but they knew that was just the way her face looked. She had on the brown plaid bucket hat she always wore, and what their father called her uniform: black pants, black turtleneck, black boots, and a tan trench coat. Maisie didn't think she'd ever seen anyone as beautiful as Mrs. Morimoro in that moment.

Mrs. Morimoro saw Maisie and Felix standing there, and her angry face turned as happy as it could.

"You two? Back home?" she said.

"Just visiting," Felix said, fighting the urge to hug Mrs. Morimoro hard.

She nodded. "So how is life in Newport? You own a yacht yet?"

"Two," Maisie said.

"One each!" Mrs. Morimoro laughed.

She motioned to the building. "Looks the same,

right? They said they were going to paint the hall, but I haven't seen anyone doing it yet."

Maisie smiled. They always said they were going to paint the hall. And change the worn linoleum. And all sorts of things they never did. If she walked through that door, she could point right to the most scuffed-up spots on the floor, and to the black marks she had left on the wall by 1C once when she'd squeezed her bike out from under the stairs. Maisie bet she could find those things blindfolded.

"Good to see you two," Mrs. Morimoro said. "Tell your mother I miss her singing."

The bus pulled up to the stop in front of the building, and Mrs. Morimoro boarded it without looking back.

Maisie and Felix watched the bus pull away and head north. Then they looked at each other. The weight of the unfamiliar key in his pocket made Felix feel sadder still. He remembered his Tintin key chain with the big front door key hanging beside the two slender keys that opened the locks on the apartment door, and found himself missing that old thing. If he still had it, he would slip the big key into this black door, then walk inside and up the three stairs to the second door, which also opened with that key. He would walk past 1A, where Mr. Soucy lived with his Scottie dog, Rebecca, and down the hall past Mrs. Morimoro's apartment with the wreath of fresh flowers she always hung on the door, right up to 1C. Felix knew that to open the first lock, you had to pull the doorknob ever so slightly, and to open the top lock, you had to release it. Once inside, he would make whoever lived there now leave. He would reclaim his childhood home.

The door opened again, and this time a girl about their own age, with curly hair and a face full of freckles, walked out. Maisie and Felix knew who lived in all three apartments on all four floors. This girl was a stranger. Which meant she lived in *their* apartment.

"Hey!" Maisie said, taking a step toward the girl.

The girl studied her closely, probably trying to decide whether the rule of never talking to strangers included strangers her own age.

"You live in there?" Maisie asked.

The girl nodded. She was skinny, and even though the weather was mild, she shivered in her

T-shirt without a jacket on. Felix saw that she even had freckles on her arms.

"In 1C?" Maisie demanded.

The girl narrowed her eyes. "Who wants to know?" she said with a southern twang.

Felix decided to intervene. "We used to live there," he said.

"When?" she said.

"Only our whole lives," Maisie said.

"Well, I wish you still lived in that dumb apartment. I wish you lived there instead of me," the girl said, surprising them by bursting into tears.

The crying, however, surprised them less than the idea that someone wouldn't want to live at 10 Bethune Street.

The girl flopped onto the stoop, and Maisie and Felix joined her, one on each side.

"I just want to go home," she said through her sniffles.

"Us too," Felix said.

At that, the girl managed to smile. "I'm Delila. Delila Monroe," she said, pronouncing Monroe with the accent on the first syllable: *Mon*-roe. "And you're Maisie and Felix Robbins, the famous twins everyone in the building loves," she added.

"So you moved here from . . . ," Maisie began.

"Charleston, South Carolina," she said dreamily.

"And you wish you were back there," Maisie continued.

"And you moved to . . . ?" Delila said.

"Newport, Rhode Island," Felix told her.

"And you wish you were back here," Delila finished. She shook her head. "Isn't life a puzzlement?"

"Do you think . . . ?" Felix began cautiously.

Delila got to her feet and wiped at her jeans. "Absolutely," she said. "Come on in."

As soon as they entered the building, the familiar smells swept over them. Felix took a deep breath, trying to fill his lungs with the wonderful scents.

"Wait a minute," he said, taking Maisie's arm. "Take a deep breath," he said.

She did. "So? It smells the same as always." She added, "Nice."

Felix walked to 1A. "Cinnamon," he said. "From all the baking Mr. Soucy does."

"Okay," Maisie said, not sure what her brother was getting at.

She watched him continue on to 1B.

"Flowers," he said, pointing to the wreath on the door.

At 1C he paused and took an exaggerated breath. "Christmas trees," he said. "From the wood Dad always cut and left by the door for the fireplace."

A look of understanding crossed Maisie's face.

"Those are the things we smell when—" She glanced at Delila and stopped herself from finishing.

"When we travel," Felix said.

"When we travel," Maisie added, "it smells like home."

CHAPTER 3

Lame Demon

As soon as Felix and Maisie walked into their old apartment, they both wished they hadn't come in after all. Even though the hallway of the first floor of 10 Bethune Street had smelled exactly the same, nothing inside the apartment was the same. Apparently, Delila's mother liked for things to match. The window that looked out on Greenwich Street and the D'Agostino supermarket used to have a bamboo shade on it. Now, heavy olive-green draperies hung over it. The living room wall was also green—"Celery!" Delila's mother told them—and all of the furniture was green, too: a green-striped sofa and a green floral overstuffed chair and just green, green, green everywhere they looked. "Green is soothing," Delila's mother said.

As if that wasn't bad enough, Maisie and Felix's old bedroom, with their twin beds separated by a scrim from one of their mother's plays, had been converted into a frilly white concoction.

"It's like we walked into a giant meringue," Maisie whispered to Felix.

She was right. Everywhere Felix looked, he saw more white, more lace, more ruffles.

Delila flopped onto her white bedspread, and for a second she seemed to disappear into all that white. But then everything settled around her, and she stared out unhappily at Maisie and Felix.

"My room at home had a magnolia tree right out the window," she said with a sigh.

Felix's eyes drifted toward the windowless brick wall, which had been painted white, too.

"Around now," Delila continued sadly, "that big old tree would be in full bloom."

"Thanks for letting us look around," Felix said, looking like he might actually run out of the apartment any second.

"Yeah," Maisie mumbled. "Thanks."

They declined Delila's mother's offer of pound

cake and made their exit. To Felix's surprise, once they got outside, Maisie burst into laughter.

"What's so funny?" he asked her. He felt so sad about the loss of their beautiful home that he couldn't believe Maisie had found anything to laugh about.

"Wait until we tell Dad what they've done in there," Maisie said.

Their father had painted their old kitchen with cartoon images of food—smiling broccoli and dancing salt and pepper shakers, fat toast popping out of a toaster, and a percolator coffeepot. Delila's mother had painted right over them in a green she called avocado.

"He'll be furious," Felix said.

Maisie shook her head, still laughing. "I think he's going to laugh as hard as I am," she said. "I mean, it's so awful."

Not sure why that was funny, Felix glumly took a seat on the uptown C train beside his sister. How could she not feel as terrible as he did about the fact that their home was really, completely gone?

When they opened the door to the apartment on

West Eighty-Sixth Street, the smells of sausage cooking and chicken baking and fresh rosemary greeted them.

"No vegetarians here, right?" a woman wearing an apron said to them brightly. The apron had a statue on it so that the woman's head looked like the head of the statue. The woman had long auburn hair that fell in perfect waves past her shoulders, green eyes like a cat, and a smile of dazzling white teeth. Agatha, Maisie and Felix realized with a sinking feeling, was gorgeous.

"I'm making the chicken I love from Orso. Do you know it? On West Forty-Sixth Street?" Agatha said. "It has sausage and olives and all sorts of yummy things in it."

"Smells good," Maisie admitted.

"It's not good, Maisie," Agatha said, flashing her shiny teeth. "It's fantastic. Just wait."

"Um," Felix said, "where's Dad?"

"Out somewhere," Agatha said, stirring some tomatoes into the pan. "Oh, Felix, I saw that your coat's buttons were hanging literally by a thread, so I sewed them for you."

"Thanks," Felix said through gritted teeth. Was

there anything Agatha *couldn't* do?

"I thought after dinner we could play Pictionary," Agatha said in her cheerful, can-do voice. "Don't you just love Pictionary?"

"Well," Felix began, but Agatha had started to hum. Beautifully, of course.

"What's that song you're humming?" Maisie asked her.

"'Crazy'? By Patsy Cline? I played her in a show a couple years ago. So tragic," Agatha said.

"You're an actress?" Felix said, feeling very possessive. Their mother had spent most of their childhood auditioning for plays and getting just walk-on parts, or—mostly—no parts at all.

"For a few years I acted, but then I went back to school for my PhD in art history, and that's how I ended up at the museum in Doha, and that's where I—"

"Met Dad," Felix said. He noticed that Maisie was watching Agatha with something like wonder. He glared at his sister, but she didn't seem to notice.

Agatha grated cheese from a hunk of Parmesan into the pan. "That's right," she said.

"Were you on Broadway?" Maisie asked.

Agatha waved her hand dismissively. "I had a few small roles. You know, *Rent* and—"

"You were in *Rent?*" Maisie asked, and the awe in her voice made Felix glare harder. Their mother had tried out for *Rent*. Three times.

"In daylights, in sunsets," Agatha sang in her beautiful voice.

Unbelievably, Maisie joined in with her.

"In midnights, in cups of coffee," they sang, Agatha holding a wooden spoon like a microphone.

From behind Felix, their father's voice rang out. "In inches, in miles," all three sang.

By the time they finished with a rousing, loud "Seasoooons of love!" Felix was ready to scream.

"Isn't she great?" their father said, grinning at Agatha.

He unwrapped a thick eggplant-colored cable-knit scarf from around his neck. "She knit this for me on the plane ride over," he said in a stage whisper.

Maisie *oohed* and *aahed* over the scarf, but all Felix could think of was their mother in her rumpled suits, lugging her heavy briefcase with papers overflowing from it.

The dinner was, of course, delicious. So was the dessert, something called tiramisu, which was Italian, too. Afterward, Maisie and Agatha beat Felix and his father at Pictionary. Then Agatha brought out a tray of chocolate truffles she'd whipped up, and took a ukulele off a shelf and played while they sang along. Felix joined in reluctantly on "Over the Rainbow," but deep down he felt melancholy. Their mother was with the boisterous Bruce Fishbaum, and their father had ended up with a goddess. *How traitorous to be won over by her charms,* Felix thought.

Finally, Maisie and Felix got to go to bed. Agatha was staying the night with her best friend Lulu in Brooklyn, but before she left she brought them water and a book of poems by Shel Silverstein.

"These are such fun," she said, placing the book on the night table between them.

As soon as she closed the door behind her, Felix said, "How can you be so nice to her?"

"What?" Maisie said through a yawn. "She's great."

"Too great," Felix mumbled.

"And I told you Dad would laugh when I told him how awful the apartment looked," Maisie said.

He had laughed. *Celery?* he'd said. *Avocado?*

"Well, I'm glad you two find it so funny," Felix said, rolling on his side away from Maisie. "I think it's terrible."

Maisie didn't answer him. Instead, she chuckled.

Felix turned back over and there his sister sat, reading those Shel Silverstein poems and chuckling to herself. Of course Agatha would choose the perfect book for them, Felix thought miserably as he faced the wall again.

The next time he rolled over, Maisie had fallen asleep with the book open across her chest. She was so hard to figure out, Felix thought. He had been certain that Maisie wouldn't like anybody their father went out with, especially someone as perfect as Agatha. Instead, she thought Agatha was great. Why, she seemed almost happy that their father had a girlfriend.

Felix sighed, wishing they were back in Newport. If they were at Elm Medona, he would try to figure out how to get into The Treasure Chest. Nothing like a little adventure to make the fact that your father has met the woman of everyone's dreams seem not so bad. He closed his eyes. The next time they went into The Treasure Chest and picked up an item, Felix thought as he drifted off, they should choose more carefully.

Obviously that hawk feather would bring them to the Old West. And if they'd looked more closely at that coin and seen the date, they would have known where they were headed. Or at least *when*.

Next time, Felix thought.

He looked over at his sleeping sister.

"Do you know what I wish?" he said, even though he knew she couldn't hear him. Or maybe *because* he knew she couldn't hear him.

"Hmmm," she mumbled.

"I wish we could time travel right now." Felix stared up at the ceiling, which was painted the color of the sky. *Blue as the sky,* he thought.

"I don't want to be here," he said softly. "I don't want to be with Agatha, and I don't want to be in Newport with Bruce Fishbaum."

"Well," Maisie said, surprising him, "would you like to be in a castle? With a moat and a jester and damsels in distress?"

"You heard me," he said, half glad that she had, and half embarrassed.

Maisie was getting out of bed now, and she looked exactly the way she did when she was up to something.

"A big castle with serfs and maybe a dragon and

lords and ladies," she said.

"What are you talking about?" Felix asked.

She went over to her suitcase, which lay open in the corner. Felix watched her rooting around until she found whatever she was looking for.

"Ta-da!" Maisie said, holding out the crown.

"Where did you get that?" he asked.

"From The Treasure Chest."

"But how—"

"Remember after that awful March Madness party?" she explained. "You found me in The Treasure Chest, right? But I had already tried to time travel by myself. I saw this and I thought that going to medieval times—you know, maybe with King Arthur and the Round Table, or someplace romantic and exciting—would make me feel better. I tried all sorts of ridiculous things to *go*.

Felix looked from his sister's face to the crown and back again.

"Are those real jewels?" he whispered.

"I think so."

"That crown is from The Treasure Chest, which means . . . ," he began.

"Yup," Maisie said.

"Maybe there will be knights," Felix said, climbing out of bed. "I would like to see real knights, and all their weapons and stuff."

He reached out to take hold of one side of the crown, but Maisie pulled it closer to her.

"Wait," she said. "I have to tell you something."

"*Now?* Can't it wait until we get back?" Felix said, frustrated. Now that he could leave Agatha and Bruce Fishbaum and his ever-changing life behind, he wanted to get on with it.

"This is kind of important," Maisie said.

"Fine," Felix said, dropping back onto the bed.

"The other day, Great-Uncle Thorne found me at the doorway to The Treasure Chest."

Felix looked at her, surprised.

"I go there sometimes to see if maybe there's a way to get in that we haven't figured out," she admitted. "Anyway, he went on and on about how dumb we are, how we don't know anything about The Treasure Chest—"

"What else is new?" Felix said, wanting her to get on with it. Already he was imagining eating big turkey drumsticks with his hands, and drinking mead—whatever mead was—while a minstrel serenaded them.

"He said that the anagram actually could help us," Maisie said.

That got Felix's attention. "How?"

"It can give us background," she said.

"You mean like we would know ahead of time who we were looking for?"

She shrugged. "He didn't really explain."

"How do we use the anagram to get background?" Felix said, feeling prickly. He wanted to *go*.

Maisie shook her head again.

"Maybe we have to just say it or something?" Felix offered. Why hadn't Maisie gotten the specifics? He knew how Great-Uncle Thorne could be, but still, she could have at least found out what he was talking about.

"Maybe," Maisie said.

She held the crown out, and Felix hurried over to her and grabbed on.

"Lame demon," they both said hesitantly.

Before they could say it again, that familiar smell of gunpowder filled the room. Then they smelled cinnamon and Christmas trees and flowers. The wind whipped around them, and they were somersaulting through time.

CHAPTER 4

Ali'i Girl

Except this time, something was different.
Very different.

Some kids like to go on carnival rides that spin around and around. Felix was not one of those kids. In fact, he didn't like spinning at all. So when instead of landing like they usually did, Maisie and Felix started to spin, he found himself not only frightened but also yelping. A yelling blur flew past him, a blur he thought might be his sister. But she went by too fast for him to be certain. And Felix was picking up speed, too. He thought he might be sick, that fancy chicken of Agatha's rising into his throat. Was this what *lame demon* had done? he wondered. Sent them out of control, unable to land?

"Feee . . . liiiiix," Maisie called, her voice warped and whirling.

"Maisie? Can you grab my hand?"

He held his hand out and his sister bumped past it. Felix saw her trying to reach him, her own hand outstretched. But just like that, she was gone again.

Palm trees seemed to fly past. And grass huts. And a man holding a large conch shell. Felix remembered something his father had told him once, a way to keep from getting seasick. *Look at the horizon. Keep your gaze on a fixed point.* Felix tried that. He stared hard at a palm tree, even as it, too, spun out of control. To his surprise, it helped. The palm tree, at least, was clear and steady.

"Feee . . . liiiix."

He heard Maisie calling, and once again he held his hand out to her. This time she caught it, and hand in hand they rode the cyclone.

"Well," she said, "*this* is fun."

It figured that his sister would actually enjoy being caught like this, in a vortex or spiral or whatever it was.

"What's out there?" Felix asked. "What do you see?"

"Nothing," she said.

"Nothing?" Felix repeated. His heart started to race again. What if they had traveled so far back in time that there were no people even on earth yet? What if dinosaurs were roaming around?

"Kind of," Maisie answered unhelpfully.

Felix could hear a sound in the distance, like people singing. No, he decided. It was just the sound of the gentle breeze. He realized he was sweating. A lot.

"It's really hot in here," he said.

"Ssshhh," Maisie told him. She heard it, too. "I think there are people over there. Chanting."

"You sure?" Felix asked cautiously. "It might be this wind."

Around them, the wind whipped and blew. Maisie strained to listen to the sounds beyond the wind. She squinted to see what was out there.

Felix was right. It was brutally hot. Even the grass looked hot. When the people chanting came into sight, Maisie forced herself to focus. A group of half-naked men sat underneath trees or on mounds of straw. They were big men—tall and bare-chested—and though they did not look especially dangerous, Maisie did not think it would be a good idea to find that out for certain. Some of the men smoked pipes; some scooped white stuff out of bowls and ate it. These men listened carefully to the ones chanting, especially the tallest of the onlookers, who stood under a tree slightly away from the others, his head cocked as if to listen better. Maisie could see the top of a thatched roof beyond the group of men.

"There's a house over there," Felix said. His voice sounded funny, like that of someone shouting down a mountain.

"More like a hut, I think," Maisie said. "A *grass* hut," she added, excited. Where in the world did people live in grass huts? She smiled to herself. And *when* did they live in them?

"So we must be on an island somewhere," Felix said, disappointed. "No knights. No damsels in distress."

"No," Maisie said, wondering what had gone wrong. A crown should take them to a castle, shouldn't it? Maybe they had somehow gone back to Saint Croix, back to Alexander Hamilton. But that didn't make sense. There hadn't been grass huts there. There hadn't been practically-naked people.

Now she saw that there wasn't *a* grass hut. There were lots of them scattered beneath the trees, windowless, with thatched roofs. The biggest one stood in the middle, near the men.

"It's like a neighborhood," she said to Felix.

Just when Felix and Maisie thought they might be caught in the tornado forever, four things seemed to happen all at the same time.

A few drops of rain fell.

A baby cried.

The men began to cheer and shout.

And the door of the big hut opened and a woman ran out, also shouting.

Everyone was pointing to the sky, ecstatic. There, stretching across the sky and seeming to drop into the distant hills, was a rainbow. Maisie had never seen one like it before. Each color glimmered in the sunlight, and for the first time ever, Maisie could actually see all seven colors, just like her kindergarten teacher had taught them: red, orange, yellow, green, blue, indigo, and violet. Each of them vivid and distinct. The rainbow formed a perfect arc in the middle. It almost looked as if someone could actually walk across it like a beautiful multicolored bridge.

"What are they saying?" Felix asked.

Maisie shook her head without looking away from the rainbow.

"They're not speaking English," she said.

Felix tried to make out what language they were speaking, but the wind suddenly grew even stronger, and lifted him and Maisie again, higher and higher. It took all his strength to keep hold of his sister's hand. Just when he thought he couldn't hold on for another second, the wind weakened again—keeping them suspended in the middle of its vortex, but allowing them to see what lay below: a bustling seaport, full of whaling ships and sailors, more half-naked native people, and westerners dressed in high-collared shirts, long-sleeved coats, and pants or skirts.

"They must be so hot in—" Maisie began.

But she was interrupted by a long, low sound that stopped all the action below.

It came from a man in a loincloth holding a giant conch shell to his lips. He blew three times, then lowered the shell and faced the crowd.

"Aloha!" the conch blower said in a deep, loud voice.

"Aloha," the crowd responded.

"I bring news of the birth today of an *aliʻi*, a girl born to Keohokālole, who will be *hanai* to Konia, granddaughter of Kamehameha the First, and High Chief Paki."

"Felix!" Maisie said, squeezing her brother's hand. "We have to pay attention. This must be the information we need."

The conch blower continued his announcement.

"Our high chiefess, Kinau, sister of our king Kamehameha and wife of the governor of Oahu, has named the baby Liliu Loloku Walania Kamakaeha."

A murmur spread among the Hawaiians in the crowd.

"Liliu's birth is auspicious," the conch blower proclaimed. "On this cloudless day, at the moment of her birth, a rainbow appeared in the sky."

Maisie and Felix looked at each other. They were there when this royal baby was born. They had seen that rainbow.

"Liliu will be important to Hawaii," the conch blower said proudly. "Let us rejoice in her arrival. Aloha!"

"Li-li-u," Felix said carefully. "That must be who we have to give the crown to."

But Maisie looked troubled. "We're in Hawaii, right? I mean, they said *aloha*, and even I know that's what they say in Hawaii."

She remembered when Bitsy Beal came back from her vacation on Maui and how every time she came in or walked out of a room she said *Aloha!* She wore a purple flower behind her ear for a week, too, and a puka shell necklace.

"You're right!" Felix said, terrified. "We're in the wrong place! And we're stuck in this . . . this . . . vortex, and—"

"You don't know it's the wrong place," Maisie said, trying to hold on to Felix and memorize the name Liliu.

"We have a crown! There aren't kings and queens in Hawaii!" Felix said, frustrated. "Hawaii's a state!"

Maisie thought about what Great-Uncle Thorne had told her. The anagram could give them information and get them out of a tough spot. Did this qualify as a tough spot? she wondered.

She looked at her brother's frightened face, and the seaport far below. Then she tried to land, to push against the force that seemed to be holding them in place. But it was impossible to move of her own will.

"We have to say it again," Maisie told Felix.

Felix thought again of castles and knights.

"You think that will get us out of here?" he asked hopefully.

Maisie realized she hadn't told her brother everything Great-Uncle Thorne had said to her, and when he found out, Felix would be really mad at her. She would just have to deal with that later.

For now, she took the crown from her inside pocket, and with some effort she managed to twist her body around to face Felix.

"Hold on and say it again," she told him.

"Lame demon," they said again as their hands gripped the crown.

The familiar smells and sounds came, and the children began tumbling through time and space.

Then, for a nanosecond, there was nothing. No sounds. No smells. No movement.

And then, with a crash, they landed.

CHAPTER 5

Liliuokalani

A girl stared down at Felix. She had a plain face and dark hair that was parted down the middle and braided.

"Where did *you* come from?" she asked him.

Felix knew he was on a beach. He could already feel sand between his toes and hear waves crashing. The girl looked Hawaiian. *Good*, he thought. *We're still in Hawaii.* All they needed to do was find this Liliu and give her the crown.

"I was sitting here watching *he'e nalu*—"

The girl, seeing his confusion, pointed toward the ocean, where tiny dots bobbed in the water.

"And all of a sudden here you are," she finished.

Her eyes brightened.

"Are you *aumakua*?" she asked eagerly.

"I . . . I'm Felix Robbins," Felix answered.

He stared past the girl. Those dots on the water were coming closer, and he could see now that they were surfers, dozens of them. The waves, ten feet tall or more, curled menacingly toward shore.

"And I've lost my sister," he added.

"But where did you come from?" the girl asked again.

Felix studied her as he tried to think of an answer. Oddly, she wore a long black skirt and a long-sleeved button-down shirt that came all the way up her neck. She even had on a black jacket, despite the heat.

She narrowed her eyes. "You are so pale, you must be *aumakua*. They pop up everywhere, and then disappear again just as quickly."

"Ghosts? Is that what au . . . au . . ."

The girl laughed as he tried to pronounce the word.

"Aumakua," she said again. "Yes. Ghosts."

"I'm not a ghost," Felix said. "But I am worried about my sister."

"Where did you leave this sister of yours?"

Again, Felix searched for an answer.

"She was right next to me a moment ago," he finally said helplessly.

A terrible thought struck Felix. He jumped to his feet and ran toward the water. The waves were gigantic. What if Maisie had landed in there? She might be struggling right now to stay afloat, or to safely catch a wave to shore. Or . . . He shook his head. He didn't want to think of all the awful possibilities.

The girl appeared by his side.

"You think she's surfing?" she asked in disbelief.

Felix turned away from the ocean for an instant. This girl was so persistent, so present. Could she be Liliu? Did *lame demon* make finding the right person this easy?

"What's your name?" he asked.

"Lydia," she said.

Disappointed, he returned his gaze to the ocean, scanning the faces of the surfers riding into shore. But he did not see Maisie among them.

Shielding his eyes from the bright sun with his hand, he nervously tried to locate his sister.

Then, suddenly, a commotion broke out on the

water, way in the distance. What had been an uneven line of surfers on their boards became a busy circle. The sounds of shouting carried across the balmy air.

The people on the beach and the surfers who had ridden waves to shore all turned. The surfers began to paddle frantically back toward the commotion.

"What's going on?" Felix asked when he reached the crowd of onlookers.

"A girl got hurt," someone said.

"Haole," someone else added.

Felix began to tremble.

"Haole?" he asked Lydia.

"Haole," she said. "Foreigner."

Without thinking, Felix joined the others who were running into the pounding surf.

"Maisie!" he called as loud as he could. "Maisie!"

Maisie opened her eyes. Everything around her was spinning and blurry, and her head throbbed. As if from somewhere far, far away, she heard her name being called. But she couldn't answer. She closed her eyes, hoping that when she opened them again things would be clearer. Where was she? And what had happened to her? As she squinted from beneath one half-opened eyelid, the world around her slowly came into focus. First, she saw Felix looking wide-eyed and terrified, his face pale and his hair sticking up at crazy angles. Then she saw two bare-chested boys peering down at her with serious expressions.

"She's waking up!" one of them said, but even though his face was close to hers, his voice sounded faint.

"Maisie?" Felix asked desperately. "Can you hear me? Maisie?"

She wanted to tell him that she could hear him, though with the ringing in her ears, everyone's voice sounded small and distant. But when she opened her mouth, only a small groan came out.

"Your head," Felix said. "You banged it pretty bad."

How had she banged her head? Maisie wondered. She tried to think, but her brain felt all cloudy and mixed up.

"Do you know where you are?" the handsomer of the two boys asked her.

Maisie shook her head slightly, which sent pain

shooting into it. She winced.

"Do you know what year it is?" the other boy asked.

"Two thousand thirteen," she croaked.

The two boys looked at each other, worried.

Felix laughed nervously. "Boy, did you hit your head hard."

"Maybe you time traveled?" the handsome boy said with a little teasing smile.

"Oh, yes," Maisie mumbled, closing her eyes again. "I do it all the time."

The next time she opened her eyes, only Felix was by her side. Things looked less blurry, but her head still ached.

"What happened?" she whispered.

Felix's face flushed with relief. "You sound better," he said. Then he frowned at her. "You got hit in the head with a surfboard."

"A surfboard?" Maisie repeated, struggling to remember. Why in the world would a surfboard fall on her head?

"We were in that weird tornado or funnel or whatever it was, and then we said *lame demon* again, and I landed on the beach, but you landed in the water, and you got hit in the head with a surfboard and practically drowned." Felix's words came out in a rush, as if he'd been waiting a long time to spill them.

"Slow down," Maisie said. She could not remember being in a funnel or even in the ocean. In fact, looking at the size of those waves, she couldn't believe she'd go in the water at all.

"I . . . I don't remember," Maisie said softly.

Felix leaned closer to her.

"Maisie, do you know that we're in Hawaii?" he asked her in a low voice. "In the 1800s?"

She let his words sink in. They must have time traveled again, she realized. But hadn't Great-Uncle Thorne sealed off The Treasure Chest?

"Remember?" Felix was whispering. "You brought a crown with you to New York when we visited Dad? A crown you took from The Treasure Chest?"

A vague memory of their father in a strange apartment floated across her mind. Then another memory, of a pretty woman by his side.

"Agatha the Great?" Felix was saying.

And: "That southern girl living in our apartment?"

And: "The conch blower?"

Felix shook her gently. Had she just fallen asleep? Maisie wondered.

"Maisie?" he was saying. "Do you still have it?"

"What?" she murmured.

"The crown!"

Maisie tried to focus on her brother's face, but her vision doubled, then blurred. What was he talking about? Southern girls and conch shells and crowns?

She felt his hands patting her fleece vest.

"It's gone!" Felix said, and his voice sounded desperate.

But Maisie closed her eyes, his voice receding into the darkness that enveloped her.

Maisie felt a cool cloth on her forehead, and then a soft voice told her that she was at Haleakala.

She looked up to see a girl at her bedside.

The girl pressed a finger to her lips, then indicated with a small nod that Felix was sleeping on a mat on the floor beside Maisie.

"Haleakala is my home," Lydia continued quietly. "My *hanai* father, Paki, is here to check on you."

"*Hanai* father?" Maisie asked, her throat dry and scratchy.

"You are in Hawaii," the girl said. "In the palace of the king."

Surprised, Maisie tried to sit up and look at her surroundings. But as soon as she did, a sharp pain jolted her skull.

"Ouch!" she said, easing herself back down.

"You foolishly went into the surf at Waikiki Beach, and you were floundering about when a surfboard crashed down on you and knocked you out. Lot saved your life," she added.

Funny, Maisie thought. The girl spoke with a clipped British accent and wore western-style clothes, but she was clearly Hawaiian.

"My *hanai* father," Lydia said again. She leaned closer to Maisie and explained, "Here we have a tradition of giving a baby away to other parents in order to improve its status and strengthen bonds between royal families."

Even though it didn't quite make sense to her, Maisie managed to nod before Lydia stepped aside and the largest man Maisie had ever seen appeared in her place. Paki stood at least six feet four inches tall and must have weighed over three hundred pounds. His hair was red and his skin was fair.

Paki smiled gently down at Maisie.

"We teach our youth that when we *he'e nalu* together, we are sharing the *nalu* of mother earth," he said, his voice lyrical and kind.

"*He'e nalu,*" Lydia interpreted. "Surfing."

"You see, youth have the opportunity to wash away their past mistakes and troubles by returning to the water, by *he'e nalu.*"

"I don't think I meant to surf—" Maisie began.

"When we surf together," Paki continued, "we become family. Therefore, you are now part of our family, Maisie. You will stay here with us until you are healed."

"Thank you," Maisie said sleepily.

Paki's laugh was more of a low rumble. "Sleep," he said. "Heal, little one."

In the two days before Maisie began to wake up, Felix stayed by her side. They were in the royal palace, a place of contradictions. Some rooms were filled with heavy wooden furniture, oil paintings, and even white linen tablecloths, crystal glasses, and heavy silver—not unlike what they had at Elm Medona. But other rooms were spare, with tatami mats on the floors and low tables where meals were eaten not with silverware but with your hands, or with hollowed coconuts for scooping poi, the thick mashed taro root that seemed to accompany every meal.

All the royal children lived at Haleakala, Felix had learned. Lydia told him that for years they had lived in a boarding school called the Chiefs' School in Honolulu that had been run by the Cookes. But the school had closed and the children had returned to the palace.

"The ones who survived," she'd added sadly.

She went on to explain that when the westerners came to Hawaii, they brought diseases with them. A measles epidemic had wiped out a fifth of the population, including her brother Moses.

"The westerners," she added, "have changed everything."

Felix had squirmed uncomfortably beneath her solemn gaze. He had felt this way before, when he and Maisie landed in South Dakota with Crazy Horse and watched the Lakota struggle to keep their land and their traditions. Was the same thing happening here? he wondered.

Ever since he and Maisie first went into The Treasure Chest and ended up in 1836 with Clara Barton, Felix had become aware of how little he knew about history, despite the As he always received in social studies. That feeling had returned again and again during his two days with Lydia and the other royal children. All he'd known before landing here was that Hawaii was the fiftieth state. But slowly he was learning that many Hawaiians did not want to be part of the United States. In fact, Lydia had told him that Hawaii had been briefly under British rule.

"We just want to be left alone," she'd said with a sigh.

Without Maisie to run his ideas by, Felix spent too much time alone, wandering the palace rooms or the courtyard outside. He worried about his sister's injury, even though the king had called in a *kahuna* to check on her. The *kahuna* had mumbled some words over Maisie, splashed her with oil, and ordered bed rest. Still, Felix wouldn't feel relieved until his sister was back to her old self.

He worried, too, about the fate of these people who had taken them in. The fate, in fact, of all of

Hawaii. For Felix knew that, despite their dissatis-faction with westerners, and the United States in particular, Hawaii was going to become a state. He had no idea when, however, because once again he'd taken history for granted and hadn't paid attention to details like that.

And of course, he worried about the crown. He grew more and more certain as time passed that it had sunk to the bottom of the ocean. Without it, he and Maisie were surely stuck here for good. Even though Felix had wanted to escape his father and Agatha the Great, he didn't want to escape *forever.* He had to find the crown.

But how? Felix asked himself over and over as he walked beneath the tamarind tree in the courtyard or sat beside his sleeping sister's bed.

A trip for the children to go bowling was planned for the afternoon. There were seven royal children ranging in age from thirteen to seventeen. They called themselves *ali'i,* which meant "royalty." All of them had lived together at the Chiefs' School and learned English there. Now they lived here at the palace. Felix had a hard time keeping straight who was really brother and sister and who was *hanai*. But it didn't seem to matter to them. "Only westerners find this important," Lot had told him when Felix tried to write it down one day.

Felix was hesitant to leave his sister's side, but Lydia's *hanai* mother, Konia, convinced him that Maisie was being well cared for. Certainly their home, Haleakala, was a lovely place to get better. There were big wraparound porches on both stories, and trees and flowers bloomed everywhere on the grounds. The air inside and out was fragrant.

As they left for the bowling alley, the oldest girl, Bernice, pointed to one of the trees, which had dense green leaves and brown pods hanging from the branches. Unlike Lydia, who was plain-looking and quiet, Bernice was one of the most beautiful girls Felix had ever seen. When she smiled, two deep dimples appeared in her cheeks. Felix was glad that she smiled often.

"That tamarind tree was planted to commemorate my birth," Bernice said proudly.

"So Paki and Konia are your *hanai* parents, too?" Felix asked her.

"No," Bernice explained, "I am their only birth daughter."

"Her mother, Konia, is the granddaughter of King Kamehameha the First," Lot said.

"Which means Bernice could be queen someday," Lydia said.

When she said that, Felix's stomach dropped. Bernice couldn't be queen without a crown, could she? And besides, that crown was meant for someone named Liliu, not for Bernice. Of that Felix was certain.

"If the Americans leave us alone," Lot was saying.

Suddenly, Felix got an idea. It was the kind of idea he would normally run past Maisie first. But since he couldn't, he plunged ahead.

"I guess every king is named Kame . . . hame . . . ha," Felix said haltingly.

This sent everyone into a round of laughter.

Lydia patted Felix's arm. "Kamehameha the Great united our islands," she told him. "His son—"

"I get it," Felix said, blushing. "Each king's son is named Kamehameha. But could someone else become queen? Other than Bernice?"

"Unlikely," Lot said.

"For example, Lydia is a high chiefess," Bernice told Felix. "Her lineage goes all the way back to high chiefs under Kamehameha the Great. Still, too many things would have to happen before she would ever become queen."

By now they had reached the busy streets of Honolulu. Felix was surprised by how changed they were from his viewpoint in the time funnel. What he had seen then were mostly thatched huts with just a few western-looking buildings, many bare-chested Hawaiians, lots of sailors, and stern-faced missionaries dressed in black. Now, all the grass huts were gone, and in their place stood houses and businesses that looked very much like the ones on the streets of Newport. There were no more native Hawaiians in their traditional clothes. Instead, they wore western clothes, although theirs had patterns of palm trees and flowers.

On Punchbowl Street, Kawaiahaʻo Church rose above all the other buildings.

"That sits on top of an ancient spring," Lot said, glaring at the church. "Our people dove for that coral at a reef, then dragged the rocks here to build a church. Some of them weighed more than a ton!"

"Look!" Bernice said. She pointed across the street to where a new storefront had a freshly painted sign reading MONTGOMERY'S.

A man with thick dark hair and a thick beard stood there, jangling keys. His bright blue eyes lit up when he saw the royal children approaching. Felix assumed he was a missionary, like all the westerners he had met here so far.

"Mr. Herman Melville," Lydia said. "Good day."

"Have you defected from the church yet?" Mr. Melville asked.

"Mr. Melville vehemently opposes the missionaries," Bernice told Felix.

Surprised, Felix asked why.

The man peered down at Felix. "They've defiled the people here, young man!" he roared. "They've suppressed all of their traditions, their culture, their sport, their very nature! Do you see that monstrosity across the street?" He didn't wait for an answer. "They used the Hawaiians to build that, and their roads, and every other thing they desire. It's a sin what they're doing."

"Mr. Melville came here on a whaler from Massachusetts," Bernice told Felix.

"I took the long way around," Mr. Melville said with a grin.

"He's been to Tahiti and just about everywhere else in the South Pacific," Lot said.

"And he sets the pins at the bowling alley," Lydia added happily.

"Not anymore, I'm afraid," Mr. Melville said, holding up the keys. "I'm now employed as a clerk for Mr. Montgomery's store here."

"Well, we'll miss you then, because we're going bowling," Lydia said.

They all said good-bye to Mr. Melville and continued to the bowling alley. Bowling, it seemed to Felix, had not changed much over time. Except for the fact that there were nine pins instead of ten, and that a man reset the pins each time, the game and the rules were the same as when he and Maisie used to go bowling at Bowlmor Lanes with their parents in New York. Still, all the time they bowled, the name Herman Melville stuck in his head. He was certain he had heard it somewhere before. But with the noise of the balls crashing into the pins, and the excited shrieks of the children, Felix could not remember where.

When the game was finished, they began to walk back to the palace, and Felix took the opportunity of their silence to put his idea to the test.

"Do any of you happen to know someone named Liliu?" he asked, certain from what he'd seen in the vortex that she was the person he and Maisie needed to find.

All the royal children stopped walking and stared at him.

"Why, you know her, too," Bernice said finally.

"I do?" Felix asked.

"Didn't you know that the missionaries made us all take English names?" Lydia asked.

Felix shook his head.

"They did," Lydia continued.

She took a step closer to Felix and smiled.

"I am Liliu," Lydia said proudly.

Despite the hot sun, Felix shivered.

He was standing just a few inches from the person he knew would someday become the queen of Hawaii.

CHAPTER 6

Restoration Day

It took almost a week for Maisie to recover. With her headaches and sleepiness, she mostly stayed in bed. All the royal children visited her, and even Paki stopped by every morning, but she grew too tired to do much more than listen to their reports about life in Honolulu and around the court. Felix split his time between sitting at his sister's side and joining the others for luaus, trips to the beach, or more bowling expeditions. Despite the friction between some of the Hawaiians and the missionaries and westerners, life here was easy. The food was fresh and plentiful, and everyone liked to have fun.

The longer Felix stayed, the more he came to understand and appreciate the concept of aloha.

Before he'd come to Hawaii, he thought the word meant just "hello" and "good-bye." But he quickly came to understand that it meant much more. It was almost a way of life. Lydia had explained to him that aloha was a way to spread goodness to other people. Letting him and Maisie stay at the palace was aloha, Felix decided.

When Maisie grew stronger and got her memory back, Felix knew he needed to tell her that he'd found Liliu. And that the crown was lost.

The first thing was easy.

"She doesn't seem very . . . I don't know . . . queenlike, does she?" Maisie said.

"I know," Felix agreed. "And not only is Bernice better queen material, she actually is the one in line. Unless a million things happen to change that," he added.

"So it's unlikely that Liliu will be queen?" Maisie asked.

He nodded. Felix could see her putting all the pieces together.

"I guess," she said finally, "that a million things are going to happen."

"I guess," Felix said with a sigh.

"Well, let's give her the crown and see what happens," Maisie said.

"Um . . . ," Felix began.

Maisie patted her inside fleece pocket and frowned.

"I know my brain got a little scrambled," she said, "but where is the crown?"

Felix should have prepared an explanation. But he hadn't. And now his sister was looking at him, waiting.

"Uh," he said. "About the crown."

"You already gave it to her?" Maisie said, still not angry.

Not yet, Felix thought.

"Nooo," he admitted.

"What then?"

"You had it," he tried.

"So?"

"And you . . . well, you landed in the ocean. With huge waves."

A shadow fell over Maisie's face.

"Felix," she said, "are you telling me the crown . . ."

She couldn't bring herself to say the words. She thought of the Pacific Ocean and how big and deep it was. She thought of the crown floating to the bottom of that big, deep ocean.

Felix met his sister's eyes.

"Maisie," he said, "the crown is gone."

The good news, Felix tried to convince Maisie— and himself—was that the shard was still tucked into the corner of Maisie's pocket.

"Big deal!" she said. "We don't even know what the shard can do. We know we need that crown to get home."

"But," Felix offered weakly, "we do still have the shard."

His sister just glared at him.

Luckily, Lydia came in then and Maisie had to at least try to be nice.

"Guess what day tomorrow is?" Lydia asked them. She didn't wait for an answer. "It's Restoration Day!" she announced.

Maisie looked confused, but Felix remembered what Lydia had told him.

"The day Hawaii got its independence back from England?" he said.

"Wait," Maisie said. "England ruled Hawaii?"

"Very briefly," Lydia explained. "Our king, Kamehameha, relinquished our islands to Britain several years ago. I remember the day so well. All of us from the Chiefs' School had to march down to the fort and watch them lower and replace the Hawaiian flag with the Union Jack. Although our hearts were broken, Kamehameha promised to win back our islands for us, and he did."

She smiled at Maisie and Felix, and although Lydia was a plain girl, that smile made her look as beautiful as Bernice.

"Every year on the anniversary, there's a big celebration. And the anniversary is tomorrow. We call it Restoration Day because it was the day our islands were restored to us," she said.

"What do you do to celebrate?" Maisie asked.

She wondered if it would be like the Fourth of July, with fireworks and parades.

"You'll see tomorrow," Lydia told them.

The next morning, the sky was not the beautiful cloudless blue it had been. Instead, low gray clouds threatened rain.

"I hope we get there before the rain starts,"

Maisie said as they climbed into a coach with Lydia, Victoria, and Emma.

The coach made its way through the crowded streets of Honolulu. It appeared that everyone was heading to the Restoration Day celebration.

By the time they reached the Nuʻuanu picnic grounds, the rain had begun. But no one seemed to notice or care. The streets were lined with people waiting for the parade that was moving toward them to arrive. And Maisie and Felix, in one of the royal coaches with three of the *aliʻi* children, were part of that parade.

The native people stood beneath the thatched roofs of two large pavilions, their arms full of flowers.

The parade was led by horses ridden by the older *aliʻi* children. The people in the parade—even the horses—were decked out in vivid yellow and red and blue, covered in ribbons and flowers. Behind the older children came their royal carriage. Maisie noticed how proudly Lydia sat, her back erect and her face composed. At the sight of them, the onlookers began to throw flowers into the carriage. Lydia unfurled the Hawaiian flag, which looked a lot like the British flag to Maisie. It had red, white, and blue stripes, and a rectangle in the upper left corner with the Union Jack in it. Lydia waved it wildly.

The carriage behind theirs was even grander. As soon as it appeared, the Hawaiians cheered so loudly that Maisie's and Felix's ears rang.

"Kamehameha!" the crowd shouted, bowing and throwing still more flowers into the king's carriage, where he sat with the queen, smiling out at everyone.

When Maisie turned around to look, she couldn't take her eyes off the king. Tall and handsome, with olive skin and a fat dark moustache, he wore an enormous cape covered in brilliant yellow feathers. But Felix was riveted by the pageantry that followed the king's royal carriage. Behind it came what appeared to be a thousand riders on horseback, all of them wearing ribbons and flowers. And behind them came a few thousand more men on horseback who were less decorated but still as colorful as all the others. Neither Maisie nor Felix had ever seen such a grand sight.

The coaches came to a stop, and Maisie and Felix joined the *ali'i* children standing in two rows.

A tall man in a yellow cape stood before them and saluted.

The name John ʻĪʻī was whispered in the pavilion with great reverence.

John ʻĪʻī dropped the cape from his shoulders, revealing the most impressive muscles Felix had ever seen. The crowd gasped at the sight of him, bare-chested and walking purposefully into an arena where twenty men holding spears waited.

"What's he going to do with those guys?" Maisie asked Lydia.

"Fight them," Lydia said matter-of-factly.

"But he doesn't have a weapon!" Maisie said.

"It's the tradition of ancient warriors," Lydia answered, never taking her eyes from John ʻĪʻī. "He must stand alone and unarmed."

"But they'll kill him!" Felix said, covering his eyes.

When the crowd cheered, he peeked between his fingers and watched John ʻĪʻī catch the first spear as if it were the easiest thing to do. The spears began to fly, aimed with great force and speed at what seemed like every part of his body at the same time. Effortlessly, John ʻĪʻī caught each spear, and flung them back with equal force and amazing gracefulness.

Felix let his hand drop from his eyes, and watched in awe as every one of the spearmen were sent from the field. As the twentieth one was driven out, everyone—even the westerners—cheered so exuberantly that the ground shook with the power of their applause and shouting.

Maisie was still trembling with a combination of fear and excitement when a guard arrived to escort the children to the royal banquet.

As part of aloha, commoners were invited to eat with the king and queen. Maisie and Felix found spots to sit on tatami mats at one of the long, low tables. They feasted on roast suckling pig and fried fish and, of course, the ever-present poi.

Licking her fingers, Maisie caught sight of the adjacent room. It was full of *haole*—westerners—sitting on beautifully carved wooden chairs at a table draped in white linen, eating from china plates with real silverware and crystal glasses.

Lydia followed Maisie's gaze, and touched her arm lightly.

"It's aloha," she said in a soft voice.

Maisie frowned. "How can it be aloha?" she asked.

Lydia just shook her head.

"Maisie," she said carefully, "my people lived happily for thousands of years before Captain James Cook arrived here in 1778. We tended our land and worshipped our gods, and we were happy. The *kahuna*—the priests—set the *kapu*, which were all the things that were forbidden, and we followed these rules. Until the foreigners came. Then, Kamehameha the Second observed the *haole* men and women sitting together and ignoring the gods' wishes, and he saw there were no negative consequences for their actions. No tidal waves or thunder or fire or deaths. So he lifted the *kapu*. When the missionaries arrived, they found my people without beliefs, struggling. It was easy to convert us," she added sadly.

Maisie tried to make sense of all she was saying.

"Do you wish the *ka* . . . *kapu* were still in place?"

"I wish my people and our kingdom weren't getting erased," she said solemnly.

Maisie wished she could reassure her. But Hawaii would become a state, and the changes Lydia feared were, indeed, inevitable.

"Some people believe it's only a matter of time

before your country claims us," Lydia was saying.

She took Maisie's hands in hers and looked her right in the eyes.

"But I can't imagine it. Hawaii a state? My kingdom gone?" Lydia paused. "Can you?" she asked finally.

CHAPTER 7

Yellow Feathers

"Sleep well," Lydia told them when they returned to the palace that night. "You won't be getting much sleep tomorrow night."

"What's tomorrow night?" Felix asked.

"We're going to Hawai'i, and I thought you might want to come along."

"Aren't we already on Hawaii?" Maisie asked.

"Hawaii is made up of eight islands," Lydia explained. "This one is Oahu. The capital, Lahaina, is on Maui. And the biggest island is Hawai'i. It's called that. The Big Island."

"Where is that?" Felix asked. He tried to hide his trepidation, but when Lydia laughed at him, he realized she saw that he was wary.

"It is very far across the ocean," Lydia said. "We will get there by canoe."

"We're canoeing across the ocean?" Felix said, panicked.

"That sounds great," Maisie said.

"Do we have to paddle the canoe?" Felix said.

"*We* don't paddle it," Lydia explained. "There are ten rowers and ten sailors who do it for us. It will take most of the night."

As she left the room, she added, "So get a good rest tonight."

Maisie loved the idea of this new adventure. Boarding a giant canoe—it *must* be giant to fit so many people—and sailing through the dark night to a different island where the king waited for them sounded like the perfect way to spend their time.

"Wow," Maisie said. "A canoe trip across the ocean with twenty people rowing for us. I kind of like being royalty."

"So it's safe?" Felix asked her.

"Oh, don't be so nervous," Maisie scolded him. "It's perfectly safe."

Felix wasn't so sure.

"Maybe we'll find the crown floating in the water," he mumbled.

"The crown," Maisie groaned. "We need to figure out how to find it."

Before Felix could agree, she added, "When we get back from the Big Island."

To Maisie and Felix's surprise, not only were they and Lydia and ten sailors and ten rowers going to Hawai'i, *all* the royal children were going. The canoe actually looked like a long, giant tree that had been hollowed out, with the ten rowers standing inside, bare-chested, paddles at the ready. Maisie and Felix found places together on the bark floor.

Felix noticed that the older kids stuck together at the prow of the boat. From where he sat, he had a clear, unobstructed view of Bernice. She had woven flowers in her hair, and as she laughed with Victoria, her dimples deepened.

His reverie was interrupted by the oldest, David, who thrust a coconut into his hands. The top had been sliced off.

"Drink," David instructed, lifting his own coconut and gulping its milk.

Felix took a big swallow and leaned back. Maybe this wouldn't be too terrible, he thought. He only hoped he wouldn't get seasick, the way he usually did.

As the canoe glided across the waves, Lydia and Emma started to weave flowers into Maisie's and each other's hair. The sky quickly grew dark, and Lydia sang a Hawaiian song in the sweetest voice Maisie had ever heard. With the fragrant flowers in her hair, and her stomach full of the snacks that got passed around, Maisie stared up at the starry sky above them.

"What a pretty song, Lydia," Maisie said. "What does it mean?"

Instead of answering, Lydia began to sing again, this time in English.

"Profuse bloom glowing as a delight, and lei for Kamakaeha," she sang.

"It's her song," Emma whispered to Maisie.

"What do you mean?"

"Konia, her *hanai* mother, wrote it for her. It's her name song," Emma explained.

Maisie knew she had heard the word *hanai* before, but she couldn't remember what it meant.

"Hanai?" she asked Emma.

"The people her parents gave her to," Emma said simply.

That's right, Maisie thought. On that day at the seaport, the conch blower had announced that the royal baby had been given to parents of a higher royal stature. And Lydia was that royal baby.

"Listen," Emma whispered to Maisie as Lydia sang, "Ka'ala wears a lei of rain and flowers . . ."

When Lydia finished her song, Emma moved closer to Maisie and whispered into her ear.

"You see, in the song Konia gave Lydia her legacy: the flowers, the rain, the mountains and valleys." Emma leaned back and sighed her dreamy sigh. "There could be no richer legacy than this."

Soon, Emma fell asleep, her head bobbing against Maisie's shoulder. All around Maisie, the sounds of sleeping children mingled with the lapping of the oars in the water. Finally, she closed her eyes, too, her mind filled with images of flowers and mountaintops, and Lydia's sweet song.

The canoe was met the next morning by people offering fruit and alohas. As each person stepped onto the beach, someone put a lei around his or her neck. Felix rubbed the sleep from his eyes. In the distance, gray smoke rose from an enormous mountain. Lot noticed him staring at it.

"Kīlauea," Lot said.

"What?"

"The volcano," Lot said, pointing to the mountain.

"Is it . . . erupting?" Felix asked. From the looks of it, that was exactly what was happening.

Lot nodded. "That's where we're going. To give offerings to Pele."

He started to walk off, but Felix asked him to wait.

"You mean, we're going into an active volcano?" Felix said.

He had not wanted to come on this trip in the first place, and now he was going to have to go to a volcano while it was erupting. He thought of the way he'd seen volcanoes erupt on TV, the tops of the mountains blowing off and molten lava spilling down their sides. Terrified people trying to outrun it. And not always succeeding.

But Lot laughed. "Not in it, exactly," he said. "We'll just hike to it and throw our offerings into the crater."

Felix swallowed hard. "But it's okay if we stay behind, right?"

"That would anger Pele," Lot said seriously. "She is the goddess of the volcano. You don't want to upset her, do you?"

He didn't wait for an answer. As Felix watched Lot walk away, he wondered what would happen if you upset the goddess of the volcano. Whatever it was, he felt certain it would not be good.

Glancing at Kīlauea again, Felix shivered. He decided not to look in that direction again for the rest of the day. Maybe, he thought, he would even be able to figure out a way to stay behind and not anger Pele.

During dinner later that day, two men, naked except for bark loincloths, sat before them and began to play the drums, banging with their palms and chanting.

From behind the palm trees, a girl appeared. Her dark hair, woven with flowers, hung down to the small of her back. Her white blouse was loose, and slipped off her shoulders as she moved. Maisie could see her hips swaying beneath her full skirt. A bracelet of shells clinked softly from her ankles.

"She is the court hula dancer," Lydia explained. "Hula," she added, "*is* Hawaii. It is the story of our creation. The story of our life."

Maisie watched, mesmerized, as the girl's hands undulated.

"The waves," Lydia interpreted.

The hula dancer's arms lifted, her hands making circular motions.

"Mountains," Lydia said.

Soon, a story revealed itself through her dance. With Lydia softly narrating for her, Maisie saw how the hula told about the eruption of volcanoes, the birth of rainbows and flowers, even love stories. By the time the girl had finished dancing, the sun was beginning to set. She placed her palms together in front of her and bowed her head slightly.

"*Mahalo*," Lydia murmured.

Maisie knew that meant "thank you," and she quietly said it, too. "*Mahalo*."

As she watched the hula dancer slip away, Maisie was glad hula had not vanished when the United States took over Hawaii. If it had disappeared, Hawaii's story would have disappeared as well.

The next morning, servants arrived leading horses for the ride up to the volcano.

"Are you ready for the ride through the jungle?" Lydia asked Felix.

"It's a jungle?" Felix said, his heart sinking.

Lydia pointed toward the volcano, partially covered in gray smoke.

"We are going straight up there, through the jungle."

"Great," Felix said under his breath as he climbed on top of a horse behind his sister.

Try not to think about jungles, he told himself as they bounced along. *Try not to think about volcanoes or the goddess of volcanoes or—*

"Look!" Maisie cried. "There's something . . . alive . . . moving around in that tree! A . . . a . . . monster!"

Everyone burst out laughing.

High in the trees, climbing among the red blossoms, the creature jumped from branch to branch.

"It *is* a monster," she said, which made everyone laugh even harder.

"That's a man," Lydia said, peering into the trees. "He's the royal feather gatherer."

Maisie blushed.

"Don't be embarrassed," Lydia told her. "How would you know? But watch him. He's smearing sticky stuff on the branches to hold the birds there when they land."

"Like Velcro," Maisie said.

"Vel— what?" Victoria asked.

"You know," Maisie said, but of course they didn't know. She shook her head. "It's an American . . . bird," she said.

"What's going to happen when a bird gets stuck there?" Felix asked, not liking the sound of this.

"Watch," Lydia said.

The man climbed down the tree and waited. Soon, a dozen birds were stuck there on the branches, flapping their wings and squawking. The man climbed the tree again and lifted each bird's wing, carefully plucking a feather from it. He took the feathers and placed them in a quiver slung over his bare chest. When he'd taken a feather from each bird, he lifted the bird from the branch and set it free. Soon, the sky above them was awash in bright yellow as the birds took flight.

"He takes the feathers for the robes of the king

and high chiefs," Lydia explained.

"I remember at Restoration Day, how the king's cape was covered in yellow feathers," Felix said.

"That's the sign of royalty," Lydia said, watching as the birds flew away.

"Since we've stopped here, why don't we have our lunch?" Bernice suggested.

Eagerly, everyone dismounted.

Almost immediately, Felix spotted beautiful red and yellow flowers growing in the forest. But as soon as he bent to pick one, Lydia came running to stop him.

"What are you doing?" she shrieked.

"Picking a flower," he said.

"If you pick them, it will rain," she said, exasperated. "And if it rains, we'll have to turn back."

"But why would it rain if I pick a flower? That doesn't make sense."

"Because these are special flowers, and if you pick them, it will rain, that's why," Lydia said, holding her arms up hopelessly.

"Okay, okay," Felix said. "I won't pick them. But honestly, Lydia, rain has nothing to do with these flowers."

She just shook her head at him. But she waited until he walked away from the flowers before she followed.

Back on the horses, within a few hours the ground turned from grassy and fern-covered to slippery black bumps lined with thin cracks.

"Lava!" Lydia announced happily.

Felix's stomach dropped. He was on a horse riding on top of lava; the very thought made him tremble. He hoped that Lydia didn't notice.

But she did.

"Don't worry," she told him. "This is hardened. And cold."

"Oh! Great!" Felix said, as if cold, hard lava was a good thing.

The ride grew bumpier on the uneven surface of the black lava. Felix held on tighter to Maisie.

"It's just lava," she said, squirming in his grasp.

"Oh, is that all?" he said, tightening his arms again.

"Ugh! What is that smell?" Maisie said.

That was when Felix realized he'd been holding his breath out of fear. He exhaled and breathed in.

"Rotten eggs," he said.

"That's the sulfur from the volcano," Lot told them. "The path gets narrower from here. We'll continue the rest of the way on foot. And be careful. The lava is getting hotter now as we near the crater."

"We're going to *walk* on hot lava?" Felix said.

But no one seemed to hear him. They all eagerly jumped from their horses and began scrambling across the lava. Felix watched as the ones in front lifted their feet quickly, the way people do when they run across hot sand at the beach. He looked behind him. If he didn't follow the others, he would be alone here. And soon it would be dark. Reluctantly, Felix made his careful way down the narrow path. With each step he took, the ground grew warmer, until he, too, was doing that funny hop-step across the black lava.

When he caught up with everyone, he saw that they were peering down at something. All of a sudden, he heard a rumble, and thick gray mud shot up from the crater, straight into the air.

Felix ducked, but the mud landed nowhere near him. Still, he stayed crouched, his arms positioned protectively over his head, watching as one of the servants distributed bananas. The offering, Felix realized. He didn't want to get closer. But he didn't want to make Pele angry. Even though he didn't believe in a goddess of fire, now that he was this close to the volcano, he decided it was a good idea to follow along. Just in case.

Maisie, squeezed between Lydia and Lot, stared through the stinky smoke and down into the wriggling, bubbling mud.

"Wait until it gets dark," Lot said. "That's when the real show begins."

She watched as he tossed two bananas into the crater.

Maisie knew that sometimes people prayed when they made offerings. Why, even when kids threw pennies into fountains, they made wishes.

She took a deep breath, her nose filling with the rotten egg smell, and closed her eyes.

"Please, please, please let us find that crown," she said, soft enough for Pele but no one else to hear.

Then she opened her eyes and threw two bananas into the bubbling molten lava below.

CHAPTER 8

Mr. Melville to the Rescue

This was what Maisie knew to be true: Back at home, in Newport and how hard it still was for her to admit that was home now—her mother was canoodling with Bruce Fishbaum. And in New York, her father was canoodling with Agatha the Great. What she didn't know was how she and Felix fit into this new world. Sometimes it was almost impossible to believe that just a year ago, her life was in place, as it had been for as long as she could remember. Other times, that old way of life seemed more real than the strange new one she inhabited. Would she ever be able to figure out how to keep what was good from before and still be able to adapt to all the changes? Maisie wondered.

At this moment, she was sitting on a veranda at the palace waiting for Felix so they could walk together into the bustle of Honolulu. While she was convalescing, he had learned his way around the busy streets. And sitting on a veranda at a palace, nibbling on fresh pineapple and gazing out at birds-of-paradise and hibiscuses and orchids was not unpleasant. Not in the least. Yet Maisie was beginning to get that urge to go home, despite all the problems waiting for her there.

Felix appeared in the garden and waved to her. His skin had browned in the sun, making his eyes seem even greener. And the salt air made his cowlick stiffer and straighter, like an antenna, Maisie thought.

"What are you giggling about?" Felix asked her suspiciously.

"Your hair," Maisie said, getting to her feet and stretching.

Out of habit, she touched the egg-shaped lump on the back of her head where the surfboard had hit her, and winced. It still hurt.

Maisie and Felix walked around the grounds, to the gate that led out to the street. The air was hot and the sun was strong, but still a soft breeze blew from time to time, cooling their skin and sending the palm trees rustling.

"So," Felix began, and Maisie knew she was about to hear a speech he'd rehearsed.

"Even though life here is pretty great," he continued, "and even though things back home are . . . in flux—"

"That's one way to describe it," Maisie interrupted.

"We still need to figure out how we're going to get back without the crown," he finished.

"Maybe this is what Great-Uncle Thorne meant when he said to use the anagram when we're in a pickle. This qualifies as a pickle, I would say."

Maisie saw the bewilderment on her brother's face.

"Oops," she said. "That's the thing I neglected to mention."

Felix stopped walking and threw his arms in the air in exasperation.

"You didn't tell me how to use the anagram the right way?" Felix said, his eyes gleaming behind his glasses.

"I did," Maisie said quickly. "Sort of," she added.

"What else did he say?" Felix insisted.

"I heard how sad you were that night back in New York, and I had the crown with me, and I just wanted to make you feel better," Maisie explained.

That was the truth, wasn't it? Even then she'd known that she should tell Felix everything Great-Uncle Thorne had said, but it was so unusual for her brother to want to time travel that she hadn't wanted to miss the opportunity.

"Maisie?" Felix asked impatiently.

"He said it would give us information—"

"I know that! You already told me. We already *did* that!" he said, his exasperation growing by the second.

"Okay, okay. He said that we could also use it if we were in a pickle. That's exactly the word he used. A pickle. Danger—"

"Thank you! I know what it means to be in a pickle, since I spend half my life in one with you!"

Felix started to walk again, his head bent, his lips moving as if he were speaking to himself. Maisie fell into step beside him.

"I think this constitutes a pickle, don't you?" she asked.

"That's what I'm trying to figure out," Felix said. "We aren't exactly in danger. In fact, we're safer than we've been other times." He thought of the ship fire with Alexander and fleeing to Shanghai with Pearl, and shivered.

"But we can't get home," Maisie reminded him.

"Did Great-Uncle Thorne happen to mention how we use the anagram if we don't have the crown?"

Maisie shook her head no.

"Usually, we both hold on to the object and that sends us back in time," he said, and Maisie knew he didn't expect her to weigh in, that he was just thinking out loud. "This time, we said . . . well, we said what we said and held on, and it sent us into that . . . funnel thing . . . and we learned where we were and who we had to give the crown to."

He paused, his face set with concentration.

"Then we both held on and said it again, and we landed—"

"Don't remind me," Maisie groaned, touching that lump again.

"—right where we needed to be."

By now they had reached the seaport. The harbor was full of ships from France and England and the

United States, and the air was heavy with the stink of whales and rotting fish.

But Felix didn't seem to notice.

"Now you're telling me that if we say . . . those words . . . again, without the crown . . . somehow we'll get the crown back?"

"I don't know," Maisie said.

"Well, I think we should try. Don't you?"

Felix looked at her expectantly.

"But Great-Uncle Thorne said not to overuse the words," Maisie said, unsure of what to do.

"What? There's more?"

"That's all. I promise. He said if we overuse them—"

"What would happen?"

Maisie shrugged. "He wouldn't tell me. He said since The Treasure Chest was sealed it didn't matter."

"Great," Felix muttered. "Now I don't know what to do."

Maisie stared off at the ships, and the buildings of Honolulu beyond them. On the docks, people were selling silk from China, and spices like cinnamon and nutmeg, and whalebone carved with pictures of ships. Felix had been down here a dozen times already. But to Maisie it was new, and she wanted to see everything.

"Let's think about it awhile," she said, eager to buy some time. "We don't have the crown, so we're not going anywhere."

"Fine," Felix said, in a way that let her know it was not fine.

"Who would have thought," Maisie said as she moved into the crowd on the dock, "that *lame demon* could cause so many problems?"

Felix didn't hear her, though. Something had caught his eye, and he was squinting in the sun to better see it.

All of a sudden, he grabbed Maisie's arm with one hand and pointed with the other.

"Look!" he said.

She turned to see what he was pointing at. A group of sailors in dirty striped shirts and bell-bottoms, their faces bearded and sunburned, their hats pushed back on their heads, were selling a heap of treasures. The sailors appeared to be guys you wouldn't want to mess with, Maisie thought as Felix pulled her closer to them. One of them had a gold tooth that sparkled in the sun. Another had an elaborately carved saber strapped to his hip. A third had a gold hoop earring dangling from one ear like a pirate. And a fourth had a bright green, blue, and red parrot perched on his shoulder, squawking.

"They look like real toughs, Felix," Maisie warned as they neared the men. "This doesn't seem like a very good idea."

Just as she was wondering why her brother, who was usually cautious and fearful, suddenly wanted to march up to a quartet of scary-looking sailors, Maisie saw exactly what he must have seen.

The treasures they were selling were laid out on a piece of yellow silk. A whale skull. Colorful paintings of a tropical garden. Cinnamon sticks.

And the crown, glistening in the sun.

"Hey!" Maisie said as soon as she could push her way through the small crowd pawing through the objects. "That's our crown!"

The sailor with the gold tooth laughed. "Not anymore it ain't," he said.

Up close, the men were even more grizzled and unkempt than they had appeared from a distance.

"Yes, it is. It's a valuable . . . I mean . . . an important family treasure."

The parrot said, "That's a good one! That's a good one!"

The parrot's sailor narrowed his eyes at Maisie. "How much is it worth to ya?" he said in a raspy, phlegmy voice.

"I don't have any money!" Maisie said. "And besides, it's mine already. You have to give it back!"

All the sailors laughed at that, and the parrot repeated, "That's a good one! That's a good one!"

Maisie glared at the parrot.

The crowd had opened to let Maisie and then Felix in, but now all the people turned their attention to the crown.

"Must be worth a thousand dollars," someone murmured.

"More," someone else chimed in.

"A thousand dollars it is!" Gold Tooth said.

"I already told you, I don't have any money," Maisie said. "And I already told you that it's mine and you have to give it back."

"That ain't the way it works," the sailor with the earring said.

"Where did you find it, anyway?" Maisie demanded.

"In the sea," Gold Tooth said.

"That proves it's mine," Maisie told him. "I dropped it in the ocean when I had an accident."

"Poor thing." Gold Tooth clucked with fake sympathy.

"Poor thing," the parrot repeated.

"Be quiet!" Maisie snapped at the parrot.

Then to Gold Tooth she added desperately, "If you don't believe me, feel the lump on my head. I got hit there and was knocked out, and that's how I lost the crown."

"And now ya've found it," he grinned, showing off that tooth.

"Exactly," she said, relieved.

"And ya've got to buy it if ya want it bad enough."

"That's . . . that's . . . preposterous!" Maisie stammered.

Suddenly, someone shoved her aside and ran past her. In a flash, she saw that the someone was Felix, crouched low. He snatched the crown, and just as the crowd gasped in unison, he ran off with it, fast.

"You little thug!" Gold Tooth shouted, scrambling to his feet.

Stunned, Maisie took off after Felix, with Gold

Tooth pounding behind her.

"Thief!" Gold Tooth yelled.

But no one tried to catch Felix. Curious faces turned to watch the boy running with the crown, a girl with a tangle of hair flying in the breeze as she tried to catch up to him, and a dirty, big-bellied, unshaven, gold-toothed sailor shouting and huffing behind her.

Felix ducked down an alley, and Maisie followed, glancing over her shoulder. Gold Tooth was still pretty far back.

Panting, she caught up to Felix, who did not even slow when he saw her.

"I. Can't. Believe. You. Took. The. Crown," Maisie sputtered between breaths.

Felix ran alongside a building, then turned the corner to face its entrance.

MONTGOMERY'S the sign above the door read.

Felix pulled the door open and finally collapsed against the wall just inside, panting for breath, the crown nestled in his arms like a football. Maisie collapsed beside him, panting, too.

"Felix!" a man said, a look of alarm on his face. "What happened?"

Felix took a gulp of air.

"Mr. Melville," he gasped. "You've got to help us."

From Mr. Melville's back office they could hear Gold Tooth banging on the now locked front door of Montgomery's.

"You little thief! You thug!" Gold Tooth shouted.

Felix took a sip of the water Mr. Melville had brought to him and Maisie, and tried to explain.

"That guy out there stole this crown. And it's ours. And he wanted us to pay a thousand dollars to get it back."

Mr. Melville let out a low whistle.

"You have to hide us," Maisie pleaded.

"Maybe we should call the police?" Felix asked, afraid that Gold Tooth might just break down the door.

Mr. Melville shook his head. "They'll take that crown," he said, "and keep it until they unravel the story."

The sound of wood splintering filled the air, followed by the too-familiar, frightening sound of Gold Tooth's heavy footsteps pounding toward them.

"He broke down the door!" Felix gasped.

Mr. Melville glanced around the office, then ran to the small window above his desk and opened it.

"I'll stall him," he told Maisie and Felix as he held out his hand to pull them through the window.

They could hear Gold Tooth opening one door after another, screaming in frustration when he found just storerooms or empty offices.

"Run," Mr. Melville hissed at them, seconds before Gold Tooth burst into his office.

"May I help you, sir?" Maisie and Felix heard Mr. Melville ask as they scrambled to their feet and began to race down the alley.

At the corner, they stopped to be sure the coast was clear. Felix thought his heart might actually pound through his ribs, it was beating so fast.

"We need to get to the palace," Maisie said. "We need to get the crown to Lydia."

"Right," Felix said, taking off again in the direction of the palace.

Maisie and Felix did not stop again until the palace appeared before them like a beautiful mirage.

We're safe! Felix thought with relief.

Just then, he felt a hairy hand on the back of his neck.

Felix peered up and up, into the angry, grizzled face of Gold Tooth.

Gold Tooth gripped Maisie by the scruff of her neck with his other hairy hand.

"I'll fix you two," he growled.

Maisie tried to wriggle away, but he just held on tighter.

He easily lifted them off their feet and gave them a little shake, then headed back toward the harbor.

CHAPTER 9

Prisoners!

"Look what I found," Gold Tooth announced when they arrived at his ship, the *Rambler.*

The deck was filled with sailors fixing nets and ropes, sharpening harpoons, and swabbing the floor. The smell of rotting fish was so strong that Maisie had to hold her breath so she didn't throw up.

"Just what we need," Earring muttered. "Kids."

He spit right on the floor, as if the very idea disgusted him.

In one motion, Gold Tooth opened both hands, sending Maisie and Felix smack onto the wet, slimy floor.

Felix was staring at fish guts swirling in the puddle of water left by the mop. He struggled to his feet, the crown still in his hands.

"That," Gold Tooth said, "is mine."

Felix held on tighter.

"This is kidnapping!" Maisie shouted at him. "And robbery!"

"Guilty as charged," Gold Tooth sneered, and he tore the crown from Felix's hands.

"Throw them in the brig," he ordered a skinny sailor, who didn't look much older than Maisie and Felix. He had a smattering of acne on his cheeks, and his pants were too big for him; he'd rolled up the cuffs so he wouldn't trip over them and looped a rope several times around his waist to keep them up.

"Come on," Skinny said to them, contorting his face into a sneer that did not make him look any tougher.

It occurred to Maisie that they could probably run away from him without too much trouble. But the steady gaze of Gold Tooth dissuaded her from trying.

Skinny shoved them in the direction of a narrow, steep stairway that led down into a dark maze of rooms.

"Keep going," he said in his fake tough voice.

Down an even narrower and steeper stairway, they descended into the bowels of the ship. It stunk even worse than the fishy deck and was as dark as the middle of the night.

"You can't leave us down here," Felix begged.

"Shut up!" Skinny yelled, giving Felix a hard push.

Maybe his toughness wasn't just bravado, Felix thought.

Skinny produced a giant key, and Maisie and Felix watched as he unlocked what looked very much like a cage.

He grinned at them, revealing two missing teeth and many more blackened ones.

"Welcome home," he said.

When they didn't move, he yelled, "Get in!"

"You've got to be kidding," Maisie said.

Skinny stuck his face so close to hers that she could see the slight beginnings of a moustache on his upper lip.

"Do I look like I'm kidding?" he said, sending a blast of onion breath at her.

Maisie shook her head.

"Now get inside!" he screamed.

Felix took Maisie's hand.

"We have no choice," he said softly.

They had to duck their heads to enter the room, if you could call it a room. Low and dark, it was more like an empty, smelly, dirty closet. As soon as they stepped inside, Skinny slammed the door shut and locked it. He peered through the bars at them and smiled.

"Might as well get comfortable," he said. "It's six weeks to Tahiti."

Maisie's legs had fallen asleep from the way she had to scrunch them under her in order to fit in the room. She stretched them as best she could, her feet sticking through the bars when she did, and shook them until she felt pins and needles.

As soon as the feeling came back into her legs, Maisie realized that her feet were touching something soft. Soft and moving. She prodded it with the toe of her sneaker, and the thing ran away.

Immediately, another one appeared. And then another one.

"Uh, Felix?" Maisie said hesitantly.

"What?" Felix said, his voice about as miserable as she'd ever heard it.

"There's something . . . I mean . . . some *things* . . . alive out there."

Felix didn't answer.

Into the silence that settled between them came the sounds of small feet scurrying and the faint squeaks of . . . of . . .

"Rats!" Maisie yelled, yanking her feet back inside the bars.

"Rats?" Felix said, proving that his voice could, in fact, sound even more miserable.

Maisie inched away until her back hit the farthest wall, which wasn't very far away at all.

Felix did the same.

"Rats," he said, shivering.

"Maisie?" Felix said into the darkness. "Do you think this qualifies as a pickle?"

They had been sitting on the cold floor for a long time, their backs pressed against the wall, listening to the rats scampering around them, and trying not to cry.

"I would say yes," Maisie said, her voice sounding small and frightened.

"Let's try?" Felix offered.

He had no other ideas. They were locked into a room on the lowest level of a ship filled with scary sailors. The crown was who knows where, and even if they could escape from here and find the crown, how would they be able to get it away from Gold Tooth again?

Before he could say anything else, the ship jolted once, then twice, then a third time.

Felix looked at his sister.

"What the . . . ?" he began.

"Uh-oh," Maisie said. "We're setting sail."

Felix grabbed her hand.

"Say it! On the count of three, say it!"

She nodded.

"One," Felix counted. "Two. Three!"

"*Lame demon!*" they said together.

And then, exactly nothing happened.

"This is all your fault," Felix told Maisie.

"My fault?"

"You didn't tell me everything Great-Uncle Thorne said, and now we're on a ship sailing to Tahiti."

Felix knew absolutely nothing about Tahiti, except that it was six weeks away from Hawaii, which meant that he and Maisie were going to be in this dirty, smelly, cold cage for six weeks. And what would happen once they got to Tahiti? He thought of angry natives with spears, walking the plank, cannibals.

Maisie's voice interrupted his thoughts.

"Maybe we should try again?"

"Why bother?" Felix said, slumping.

"We can't just sit here," Maisie said.

Felix didn't answer. What was there to say?

"On the count of three?" Maisie asked him.

"Leave me alone," Felix grumbled.

They sat in the darkness in silence as the ship moved farther and farther into the Pacific Ocean.

"Pssssst."

Maisie opened her eyes.

"Pssssst."

She waited for her eyes to grow accustomed to the pitch black. Outside the bars, a face slowly took form.

Skinny.

"I brought you something," Skinny said.

"What? Bread and water?" Maisie said. That was what prisoners ate in the movies.

"No," Skinny said. "This."

He was holding something up for her to see, but she couldn't make it out.

"I really can't come any closer," Maisie said. "There's . . . rats running around out there."

Goose bumps ran up her arms and legs at the very thought of those rats.

Skinny snorted.

"You afraid of a rat?" he said, all full of that braggadocio.

"I bet you are, too," Maisie said.

"Am not!"

"Humph."

Skinny sighed.

"I used to be," he admitted. "When I first sailed, I spent all night scared rats would eat me up."

"Do they eat people?" Felix asked.

"Nah," Skinny said. Unconvincingly, Felix thought.

"What did you bring us?" Maisie asked, squinting toward the thing he held.

Skinny pressed his face to the bars.

"The key," he whispered. "I'm going to let you out."

Both Felix and Maisie crawled to the bars.

"You are?" Felix said, trying not to be too hopeful.

"Here's the thing," Skinny said. "The men will all be eating in about twenty minutes. While they're in the mess hall, I'll lead you to the crown."

"But then what?" Maisie said. "We're out at sea. Where will we go?"

"Look," Skinny said. "We ain't got much time. Just follow me."

The most beautiful sound Maisie thought she'd ever heard reached her ears: the key turning in the lock.

Then the door creaked open, and Maisie and Felix stepped out of their prison.

Climbing the steps from the lowest floor to the next one, Maisie and Felix had trouble walking as the ship swayed from side to side. As they reached the top of the stairs, they heard the noisy voices of the sailors sitting down to eat. The smell of roasted meat floated through the air, reminding them of how hungry they were.

But there wasn't time to worry about their stomachs now. They had to get the crown before Gold Tooth—or anyone else—finished dinner.

Skinny put his finger to his lips. "Ssshhh."

Then he motioned for them to follow him through the maze of rooms.

At last they reached a large room filled with bunks made of rope. The beds hung from hooks, like hammocks.

Skinny pointed to one along the far wall.

There, poking out of a pile of clothes, Felix saw the crown.

Quickly, and as quietly as he could, he half tiptoed, half ran across the sloping floor toward Gold Tooth's bunk.

The ship seemed to slip out from under his feet with every step, and Felix finally used the bunks for balance, grabbing the ropes that held one to the hooks and then swinging to the next one, until at last he reached the crown.

Maisie and Skinny motioned for him to hurry.

Using the same technique, Felix made his way across the room, the crown safe in his arms.

Skinny led them up the next flight of stairs, pausing to keep his balance each time the ship tacked sharply left or right.

On deck again, Maisie took big, deep breaths of the salty night air. Above them, the sky was heavy with stars. She thought if she reached hard enough, she might actually touch them. The full moon lit up the night like a streetlight, making their path clear and bright.

At the edge of the ship, Skinny stopped.

"You'll have to do this next bit on your own, I'm afraid," he said apologetically.

Felix swallowed hard. *This next bit* seemed to involve something over the side of the ship, where Skinny was now leaning and tugging on something.

"You just need to climb down—" he was saying.

"Climb? Down?" Felix repeated, glancing overboard at the roiling waves below.

"And get into this dinghy here that I'm freeing up for you."

"And . . . row? Across the ocean?" Felix asked in disbelief.

"We're not that far out to sea," Skinny said. "Yet. That's why you've got to get moving."

"I don't know," Felix said.

Not only was it a long way down to that dinghy, but once they had set off, how were they supposed to know where to go?

Skinny stopped long enough to say, "You don't have much choice, do you?"

The ropes slapped against the side of the ship, and the little dinghy bounced free.

"Off with you two now," Skinny said.

They would have to climb over the railing and shinny down the side of the ship, holding on to the ropes until they reached the dinghy that bobbed in the water below, looking very much like a toy boat.

Maisie took a deep breath.

"It's now or never," she said, and swung her legs over the railing.

Reluctantly, Felix followed.

Skinny stood above them, watching to be sure they were safely off.

"May I ask you something?" Maisie asked before she began to climb down a rope.

Skinny nodded.

"Why did you decide to help us?"

He shrugged. "I can't really say. I just . . . *had to.*"

Maisie glanced at her brother. His face was wrinkled with fear and concentration, but she wondered if he, too, thought *lame demon* had saved them.

Hanging from a swinging rope far above the ocean, Felix wished he had gone on that rock climbing field trip last winter. But it had been optional, and Maisie had refused to even consider it.

An hour on a bus with Bitsy Beal and her posse just to climb a wall all day? No thank you. Felix had thought it would be fun—the bus ride and the day at the rock-climbing gym and stopping for fast food on the way home. But he couldn't leave Maisie alone, could he? So he hadn't gone, either, and now he was sorry.

Every now and then the ship moved in such a way that he banged against the side, hard, then swung out far from the ship, dangling for an eternal few seconds over the water before gently swinging back into place.

Slowly, slowly, he inched down the rope, squeezing his eyes shut most of the way.

He heard when Maisie reached bottom and dropped into the dinghy with a little "Oh!" followed by the sound of the dinghy rocking in the waves, then settling again.

"You're almost there!" Maisie called to him.

Felix peeked out from beneath his eyelids. It didn't look almost there to him. He squeezed his eyes shut again, and continued his slow way downward.

Finally, he reached the bottom. The water was right below him. Maisie waited in the dinghy, holding it steady and close with its final tether to the ship. All Felix had to do was let go of his rope and make the short jump into the dinghy.

Felix took a breath.

He let go of the rope.

And he dropped, missing the dinghy and falling right into the ocean.

CHAPTER 10

At Sea

Felix had read somewhere that just before people died, their lives passed before them, almost like a home movie. When he dropped into the ocean with a soft plunk and fell deeper and deeper, he thought first of the warm turquoise Caribbean, and then of his big bathtub at Elm Medona, and then of the Carmine Street Pool where he and Maisie used to swim, and finally of the old bathtub back at Bethune Street with its cracked white porcelain and the rust stain around the drain that nothing could remove. And as these thoughts rushed through his mind like he'd hit the REWIND button on a DVD player, Felix thought, *Uh-oh.*

He opened his eyes. Unlike the Caribbean, this

water was dark and cloudy. And so deep that it seemed like there was no bottom. Felix kicked. Hard. And pushed upward with all his might. Above him he saw the rocking shadow of the dinghy, and ripples from the paddles hitting the water.

Slowly, he began to move toward the surface.

Just when he thought he wouldn't be able to kick for even one more second, a circle of moonlight appeared. Felix aimed for it with a final burst of energy, and broke the surface, sputtering and gasping for air.

Immediately, Maisie grabbed him and pulled him into the dinghy with her.

Instead of letting him go, though, she held on, her head on his wet shoulder.

"I thought you drowned," she cried. "I thought, I thought . . ."

Felix wanted to comfort her, but he was too busy catching his breath.

The dinghy still sat in the shadow of the *Rambler*, and once Maisie got control of herself, she picked up the paddles and started to row. In the moonlight, her face looked pale and splotchy from crying.

"I'm okay," Felix finally managed to say.

Maisie just shook her head.

"What a dope I am, right?" he said, shaking his head.

Maisie stopped rowing and looked at him, her face solemn.

"I don't know what I would do without you," she said matter-of-factly.

She began to row again right away, as if the matter was closed. But Felix reached over and patted her hand.

"Me neither," he said.

He took one of the paddles from her, and silently the brother and sister rowed the small dinghy into the deep sea.

At sea, it is hard to gauge how much time has passed. Felix's arms ached and he could feel his face getting sunburned. Still, they had to keep rowing. What choice did they have? Even as the waves grew rougher and choppier, he paddled, trying to keep the dinghy on course. But the waves got bigger, and the little boat seemed to not move at all, no matter how hard Maisie and Felix paddled.

Their hair grew wet and stiff from the salt spray. The dinghy rocked, tipping precariously closer and closer to the water.

"Hold on!" Maisie shouted.

She clutched the sides of the slippery boat. Felix did the same.

He watched a wave approach from right in front of them. It was enormous, a moving wall of churning gray water.

"Look out!" he screamed.

The wave swept over them, knocking both Maisie and Felix out of the boat and turning the dinghy upside down.

Maisie coughed, spewing salt water from her nose and mouth. Panicked, she swam to the dinghy and threw herself onto it, all the time scanning the surface of the water for her brother.

"Felix!" she yelled.

For a moment, nothing.

Then Felix, too, emerged.

"Over here!" she called to him.

With great effort, Felix made his way to Maisie.

"We have to turn the boat over," she told him.

As quickly as it had come, the squall ended. The ocean was as flat as a piece of glass now, not a wave in sight. Maisie and Felix didn't calm as fast, though. Their hearts raced as they searched the horizon for another rogue wave. But none came.

Felix rested on the dinghy, trying to catch his breath. Trying not to think about sharks.

Slowly, his breath evened. He looked at Maisie and nodded.

With their last bit of energy, Maisie and Felix managed to flip the boat over and crawl back into it.

Felix didn't want to say it aloud, but he felt pretty certain that their pickle was getting worse, not better.

"Felix?" Maisie said softly.

Too tired to answer, Felix just looked at her.

Maisie swallowed hard.

Then she said, "Where's the crown?"

Felix didn't even have to check his inside pocket. The crown was heavy enough that when it was there he felt its weight, and it was big enough to be bulky.

He glanced at the ocean, which seemed to be getting vaster by the second.

"I am trying really hard not to cry right now," Maisie said, her voice sounding strangled.

After all they'd been through, now they'd lost the crown once more.

"We'll never find it again," Maisie said hopelessly.

Felix just kept staring at the ocean, as if the crown would magically appear. He watched a colorful fish caught in some seaweed in the distance.

"Wait a minute," Felix said. "That fish . . ."

"I don't care about a stupid fish," Maisie said. "We're never going to get back to Hawaii. We're never going to get home, either."

She had never wanted to be in Newport so badly before, but now she longed for her pink bedroom and the sound of her mother's heels clicking down the long hallway. She even missed Great-Uncle Thorne roaring at them.

"That fish," Felix said again, his voice growing excited.

"What's so special about that fish?" Maisie said crossly.

"That fish has the crown!" Felix announced.

He picked up the paddles and rowed toward it.

Sure enough, the colorful fish caught in the seaweed held the lost crown.

Maisie scooped it up and shook the water from it.

"Good as new," she said with monumental relief.

Maisie and Felix curled up together to rest, the crown safely back in Felix's pocket. The dinghy floated along on the current as they slept. When morning came, they woke and began to row again. Although they were both hungry, and thirsty, and scared, neither of them complained. There was no sign of land, just ocean as far as they could see in every direction. Felix wondered where they might land, *if* they made it to land. Hawaii, he'd learned from the royal children, was thousands of miles from any other land.

It was possible, he realized as his paddle slapped the water, that they would starve to death or get capsized by a wave or suffer some other dreadful fate long before they reached land. Felix glanced at Maisie. Was she having the same catastrophic thoughts? Or was she somehow confident that they would find their way back to Honolulu? He couldn't tell by her expression, which revealed nothing.

The sun climbed in the sky. When it was directly overhead, Maisie said, "Lunchtime!"

"I'll make grilled cheese," Felix said.

"I'll bake chocolate chip cookies," Maisie added.

They smiled sadly at each other.

"Let's take a break?" Felix suggested.

Relieved, Maisie put down her paddle.

"How deep do you think this water is?" she asked, peering over the edge of the dinghy.

"Don't even think about it," Felix said.

Maisie squinted. Blinked. Squinted again at something in the distance.

"I think I see a ship," she said carefully.

Felix looked, too, but saw nothing. Was she hallucinating? Seeing a mirage?

"It's coming this way," she continued. "But slowly."

"Maisie," Felix said, picking up her paddle, "I'll do the work for a while. You rest."

Maisie laughed. "You think I'm bonkers, don't you?"

"No!" he said quickly.

She pointed toward the horizon.

"Let's just hope we haven't paddled in a big circle and that it's not the *Rambler*," she said.

Now Felix squinted and blinked. Sure enough, a ship came into focus in the distance. And sure enough, it was moving slowly toward them.

It seemed to take forever for the ship to come

close enough for Maisie and Felix to see its name: *Gloria Jenny*.

Maisie began to wave her arms wildly and to shout for help.

Way up in the ship's crow's nest, a sailor stood lookout. But did he see the tiny boat with the two lost children in it?

"Over here!" Felix yelled.

It was impossible to tell if the man up there heard them or saw them. The ship continued its slow movement.

"Help!" Maisie kept shouting. "Help!"

For an instant it appeared the ship was going to sail right past them. Then, without warning, it cut sharply and headed directly for Maisie and Felix.

They did not stop shouting and waving until the *Gloria Jenny* pulled up right alongside them and the sailors staring down at them dropped a rope to hoist them up.

"What in the world are you two doing out here in a dinghy?" the captain asked as soon as Maisie and Felix were on deck.

They looked at each other, and then at the captain.

"Trying to get to Honolulu," Maisie said.

The captain grinned.

"Then you're in luck," he said. "That's where we're headed, too."

The ship was a whaler from New Bedford.

"The city that lights the world," the captain said proudly.

And it was full of whale blubber. Back in New Bedford, the blubber would be turned into oil for lamps. The captain gave Maisie and Felix a bit of it to chew on, like gum. To be polite, Felix tried, but the overwhelming fishiness of it was too gross for him, and when the captain looked away, Felix spit it out.

These sailors, unlike the ones on the *Rambler*, were a jolly crew. They took turns sitting with Maisie and Felix and telling them stories of their adventures catching whales in the South Seas. They showed them the harpoons they used, and explained the best way to throw them.

"You should have been there," one sailor said, looking dreamily off in the distance. "We harpooned this huge whale, and he took us on a Nantucket sleigh ride like I've never been on in my life."

"A sleigh ride?" Maisie asked. "In the ocean?"

The sailor laughed. "That's what we call it when we harpoon a whale and she takes off, dragging the ship along with her."

Felix smiled at the idea. He would have to remember that one. A Nantucket sleigh ride.

Another sailor brought over a small piece of whalebone and showed them how he carved a picture into it.

"Scrimshaw," he said. "That's what it's called. And I'll give this to my wife when I get back home. She'll turn it into a brooch."

The picture was of a ship on the ocean just like this one.

"You two are from Newport, I heard," he said.

"That's right," Felix said.

"Have you seen the widow's walks on top of houses by the water there?" the sailor asked.

"I don't think so," Felix said.

"Oh," Maisie said, "do you mean those little things on the roofs?"

"Right," the sailor said, nodding. "The wives go up there to watch the sea for our ship's return."

"Why is it called a widow's walk?" Maisie asked him.

The man's smile faded. "I'm afraid too often the ships don't return."

"And then the wives—"

"That's right," he said. "They become widows."

He went back to his careful carving. "She'll like this, my wife will," he said softly.

Honolulu finally appeared before them.

The crowded harbor was cast in the glow of the setting sun, everything washed in a lavender haze.

Of course, Felix had known that the sun set in the west and rose in the east, but it wasn't until he'd watched the sun set over the ocean here that he really understood. The sky turned a dozen shades of purple and red, and the sun began to drop like a fiery red ball in the sky. In an instant, it disappeared beneath the horizon, and evening fell over Honolulu.

The *Gloria Jenny* pulled into Honolulu just before that happened. The sky was all those shades of purple, and the sun was red and low above the horizon.

"You two have somewhere to go?" the captain asked Maisie and Felix.

They nodded.

"Thanks for the ride," Maisie told him.

Felix and the captain shook hands.

"Godspeed," the captain said.

Felix and Maisie walked off the ship and into the bustle of Honolulu, toward the palace, the crown heavy in Felix's pocket.

Liliu was moving across the lawn when Maisie and Felix reached the palace.

She looked excited to see them.

"Aloha!" she called to them.

"Aloha," they answered.

"You're just in time for the fireworks," Liliu said, beaming.

"What are you celebrating?" Maisie asked.

"Bernice's engagement," Liliu said. She lowered her voice. "She's marrying a *haole*, so Paki is furious. Still, he arranged the fireworks."

She motioned for them to follow her around the corner, where all of the *ali'i* sat, staring up at the sky expectantly.

"I'm sorry," Felix blurted as soon as they sat down. Liliu looked at him, confused.

From the distance came the sound of explosions.

"For what's happening here," Felix continued. "In Hawaii."

The sky lit up then. Blue and green and red. Not like the pyrotechnics Maisie and Felix were used to, but the colors were still vivid as they splashed across the sky. The air smelled of smoke and sulfur.

"The way the British and the Americans are taking over everything," he added.

"I am, too," Liliu said softly.

The three of them watched in silence as the fireworks lit up the sky.

When the fireworks ended, the crowd of revelers applauded wildly.

"Our parents," Maisie said, "they got divorced. And this whole year all I wanted was my old life back. I know it's different," she continued, embarrassed, "but I know a little bit what it feels like to try to hold on to a way of life."

Felix said, "To hold on when, really, everything is changing."

Liliu looked at them, her face solemn.

"Don't let go," she said. "Always remember the old ways, and what you've lost. If you don't keep it alive, who will?"

Maisie nudged Felix with her elbow.

"Right," he said.

He pulled the crown from his pocket.

"We brought this for you," he told Liliu.

"It's beautiful!" she said, taking it and turning it around and around in her hands. "But why are you giving it to me?"

Maisie and Felix looked at each other.

"It's yours," Felix said finally.

Maisie had a strong urge to hug Liliu, but just as she reached her arms out toward her, she and Felix were lifted into the air. And even before they were aware of the smells and sounds around them, they knew: They were going back.

CHAPTER 11

The Shard

"You guys still awake?" their father was asking from the doorway.

Maisie and Felix looked at each other.

"Uh . . . yeah," Maisie managed to answer.

"Want some ice cream?" their father said.

Felix couldn't answer. He was still seeing Liliu's face, her braids hanging down her back, the sky behind her still smoky from the fireworks. He was still smelling the hibiscuses and orange blossoms and orchids.

"Sure," he heard Maisie say.

"Come on out to the kitchen," their father told them.

He was looking at them oddly.

"Are you two up to something?" he asked.

That was exactly what Mom would say, Felix thought. And that thought made him almost cry. Why couldn't his parents see how alike they were? How right they were for each other?

His parents had gotten married at City Hall with a small group of friends by their side. They had an ivory photo album filled with snapshots, his mother wearing a white shift dress, grinning up at his father, who stood beside her in his trademark blue jeans and a white button-down shirt with a brightly colored tie. They looked happy in those pictures, Felix always thought. It was a sunny June day, and his mother clutched a fat bouquet of yellow sunflowers. After the ceremony, the wedding party had gone to Chinatown and eaten themselves silly at Wo Hop. There were pictures of that, too: his parents holding chopsticks and feeding each other broccoli and dumplings; opening a bottle of champagne, the foam dripping down his father's hand; his father's arm casually draped over his mother's shoulder as he made a toast. In all of them, there was no sign that their love would ever end, that they would get divorced and find new people to love.

In the kitchen, their father pulled out cartons of ice cream: Cherry Garcia and Phish Food and New York Super Fudge Chunk.

"Why so glum?" he asked them.

Felix just shook his head.

But Maisie said, "We miss us."

"Us?"

She nodded. "Our family. *Us*."

Their father scooped a ball of each flavor into the bowls. That's how they did it in their family.

"So do I," he said at last. "So do I."

The next morning, Maisie and Felix had to go back to Newport. They kind of wished that Agatha the Great wouldn't be there for breakfast with them and their father, but she was. She arrived fresh from Pilates, her hair in a ponytail, and a purple yoga mat sticking out of her oversize bag.

They had asked their father if they could have their last breakfast of the trip together at the Bus Stop Cafe, the very ordinary diner on the corner of Hudson and Bethune Street, where they used to go for grilled cheese sandwiches on lazy afternoons, or plain old bacon and eggs on mornings when they ran out of milk or just felt like having someone else scramble the eggs. *You really want to go there?* their father had asked. He'd offered them all kinds of special breakfasts—knishes at Schimmel's, Goldilocks omelets at Sarabeth's, dim sum in Chinatown—but the only breakfast Maisie and Felix wanted was at the Bus Stop Cafe.

"Isn't this cute?" Agatha said when she arrived.

Maisie noticed how she squeezed their father's hand and bumped her shoulder against his.

"It's not cute," Felix said. "It's just regular."

"Okay," Agatha said, giving their father a look that neither Maisie nor Felix could read.

"The coffee is pretty bad," their father warned her.

"No," Maisie reminded him. "It's not bad. It's serviceable."

That's what he always used to say. *The coffee isn't terrible, Jenny. It's serviceable.* And their mother would wrinkle her nose and take a sip and say, *You are absolutely right, Jake. This is a cup of serviceable coffee.*

"Okay," Agatha said again.

Their father took a swallow of coffee and nodded.

"Thank you for reminding me, kiddos. This is indeed serviceable coffee."

"Inside joke, I guess," Agatha said.

They ordered. Egg-white omelet for Agatha. Bacon and eggs for the three of them. With white toast. Their mother always said that the only thing white bread was good for was toast.

"So," their father said as he mopped up the last of his egg with the last of his toast.

Maisie's stomach rolled. Something about the way he said *so* let her know he was about to make an announcement. She hadn't heard a good announcement in almost a year, ever since that day when her parents told her and Felix they were getting divorced.

"What would you two say if I told you I was moving back to the States?" her father said.

Maisie shook her head as if to clear out any interference. If her father was leaving Qatar and moving back, then this was a very good announcement.

"I would say great," Felix said.

"Then I guess you need to say great," their father said, beaming.

"Great!" Felix said, so happy he thought his chest might burst.

Then their father draped his arm around Agatha's

shoulders, the way he did with their mother in the wedding album.

"And what would you say if I told you that Agatha and I are going to get married?" he asked.

Agatha was grinning and their father was grinning, but Maisie and Felix's expressions had turned to stone.

"That's great, too, isn't it?" Agatha said, her voice so cheerful that Felix thought he might actually cry.

"It is great," their father said, filling the silence Maisie and Felix had left. "I'm going to rent a studio downtown again and get back to painting, and Agatha will work at a gallery . . ."

The sound of his voice spinning all the plans he and Agatha had made turned into an annoying buzz in Maisie and Felix's heads. Felix thought of Liliu, standing on that wide lawn beneath all those stars. It was their job, she'd said, to hold on to all the past had given them. How easy it was, Felix thought, to throw it away.

Soon they were on the subway to Penn Station, Agatha talking about places where they might get married and their father grinning and saying *Isn't*

that great? about everything.

And then they were on the platform at Penn Station, the train chugging noisily to a stop. Their father easily carried both of their bags onto the train, and settled them into seats on the right-hand side so that they'd be sure to have a view of the ocean when they passed through Connecticut.

And then he was kissing them both good-bye, murmuring about how by June he would be living in New York City again and they could come to visit him all the time, maybe even for the whole summer.

And then he was gone and the train was pulling away. Maisie and Felix looked out the window and found their father standing on the platform, his arm around Agatha, both of them waving good-bye.

Felix picked up the book Jim Duncan had given him. *Moby-Dick.* He stared down at the cover. There, beneath the title, was the author's name: Herman Melville.

"Maisie," Felix said, holding up the book. "Herman Melville."

"The guy who hid us from Gold Tooth?" she said.

Felix nodded. You never knew about people, he thought, opening the book.

Back at home, it seemed nothing had changed.

The Treasure Chest remained sealed. Great-Uncle Thorne spent all his time with Penelope Merriweather, and their mother spent all her time either at work or with Bruce Fishbaum.

School started up again, uneventfully.

The entire sixth grade, both Miss Landers's and Mrs. Witherspoon's classes, had to choose topics for research papers.

Felix decided on his immediately: whaling in the nineteenth century.

Maisie chose hers right away, too: the Kingdom of Hawaii.

"What are you doing yours on?" Felix asked Lily Goldberg at lunch that day.

The spring air still had a chill to it, but the sun was bright and the leaves shimmered a beautiful green beneath it. Felix and Lily had taken their lunches outside to eat.

"I'm not doing one," she said.

Lily Goldberg looked especially pretty today, Felix thought. Her dress had a pattern of apples and pears, and her hair was poking out at funny angles.

"You have to do one," he told her.

He was going to tell her about scrimshaw and Nantucket sleigh rides and widow's walks, but the way she was looking at him made him pause.

"I'm moving," she announced flatly. "To Cleveland, Ohio."

To Felix, Cleveland, Ohio, was as far away as South Dakota or Hawaii. Too many miles separated it from Newport, Rhode Island.

"Oh," he said, because that was the only word that managed to escape his throat.

"My father got transferred," she said.

"Oh," Felix said again.

They sat silently, side by side, Felix chewing his turkey sandwich, and Lily munching on slices of pepperoni.

"I'm going to miss you," Felix said finally, a familiar ache growing in his gut, the one that came with bad news: his parents' divorce, the move here, Great-Aunt Maisie's death.

Lily Goldberg stared straight ahead.

"I'm going to miss you, too," she said.

Felix saw a tear in the corner of her eye.

"We'll e-mail all the time," he said.

"People always say things like that," Lily said. "But they don't really do it."

"It's up to us to do it," Felix said. He thought about Liliu and added, "If we don't keep the past alive, who will?"

Lily finally turned to him. She grinned, her breath all spicy and pepperoni-smelling.

"You're so weird," she said, and squeezed his hand.

After dinner that night, Great-Uncle Thorne cornered Maisie and Felix in the Library.

Spread out on the table Phinneas Pickworth had brought back from Morocco was a map of a whaling route through the South Seas, the CliffsNotes on *Moby-Dick*, and photocopied pictures of whaling ships. Felix had circled one of them—the ship with the name *Gloria Jenny* on its side. Maisie sat curled up on the sofa that Great-Uncle Thorne called a divan, reading the book *Hawaii's Story by Hawaii's Queen*.

"How did you do it?" Great-Uncle Thorne demanded.

Felix, glum from Lily's news, wanted nothing less than to have to listen to Great-Uncle Thorne.

"Do what?" Felix said. "We're working on our research papers."

"Poppycock!" Great-Uncle Thorne bellowed. "Don't play innocent with me! My bones don't ache, my arthritis is gone, and my appetite is enormous."

He glared at them from beneath his impressive white eyebrows.

"In other words," he said, "you got into The Treasure Chest."

"No, we didn't," Maisie said without even bothering to look up from her book.

Great-Uncle Thorne waved his jade-tipped walking stick in the air.

"You two time traveled!" he boomed. "My beloved is over one hundred years old. Do you think I want to lose her? Do you think I want to watch her wither away?"

They didn't respond.

"It's a waste," Great-Uncle Thorne muttered. "You two don't appreciate it. You don't even use it correctly."

"That's what you think," Maisie said, placing a finger in her book to hold her place. "You told me about *lame demon* and we used it, just like you said."

"We said it and got lifted into this tornado thing, and then we landed right where we were supposed to," Felix told him.

"And it rescued us when we got into a pickle," Maisie added.

"But how did you get into The Treasure Chest?" Great-Uncle Thorne said, furrowing those impressive white eyebrows.

"We didn't have to get inside," Maisie said. "I took an object out and we used it."

"Aha! You little . . . little . . . ruffian! Do you have other objects?"

"No," Maisie admitted.

Great-Uncle Thorne stared at them hard.

"I'm not sure I believe you," he said.

Maisie opened her book again and started to read. But she couldn't concentrate, not with Great-Uncle Thorne standing there huffing and puffing.

"I want the shard," he said.

"What?" Felix asked, surprised.

"No way," Maisie said.

"I can't trust you two," Great-Uncle Thorne said. "The only way I can be sure you stay put is to take the shard."

"We're not going to give it to you," Maisie said.

"You . . ." Great-Uncle Thorne shook his fists at her in frustration. "You imbeciles! You don't even know what the shard can do. The Treasure Chest is wasted on the likes of you two."

"Why don't you tell us then?" Felix asked Great-Uncle Thorne.

Great-Uncle Thorne laughed.

"It's almost worth reopening The Treasure Chest just to watch you flail about," he said.

He grew serious again.

"Almost," he said. "But not quite."

With that, he strode out of the Library.

Maisie and Felix watched him disappear, then looked at each other.

"The shard?" Felix said.

Maisie held it up so they both could examine it.

"What in the world can this little piece of porcelain possibly do?" she wondered out loud.

The wind seemed to grow stronger, rattling the windows and whistling through the trees.

In a way, Felix hoped Great-Uncle Thorne wouldn't unseal The Treasure Chest.

In a way, Maisie hoped he would.

Queen Liliuokalani

September 2, 1838–November 11, 1917

Liliu Kamakaeha, later known as Queen Liliuokalani, was born on September 2, 1838, in a grass thatched-roof hut at the base of Punchbowl Hill on the island of Oahu in Hawaii. The hut was the largest one in a high chief's compound. Her mother, Keohokālole, was the descendant of high chiefs, and her family of court chanters and composers awaited the birth of her third child by telling of the impressive family's genealogy and deeds. Liliu's father, High Chief Kapaʻakea, came from a family of mostly warriors.

The birth of an *aliʻi*, or royalty, was believed to be accompanied by the heavens sending a signal, such as thunder, lightning, or rain. But the day of Liliu's birth proved to be unrelentingly hot and inauspicious until the moment of her birth, when it was reported that a cry came from inside the hut at the same time that one came from outside. The cry from inside announced the quick birth of Liliu; the cry from outside came when, after a few drops of rain fell, a rainbow appeared in the sky, a fitting signal of the birth of an *aliʻi*—already promised as the *hanai*, or adopted daughter, to the granddaughter of King Kamehameha I—and of a baby who would grow up to become the last queen of Hawaii.

When Liliu was born, Hawaii consisted of a kingdom of eight islands ruled by Kamehameha III. In 1778, when Captain James Cook first sailed into Hawaii, there was a population of three hundred thousand on the islands. White settlers brought new diseases like measles and smallpox with them, and by 1838 the population had dwindled to only forty thousand. Eighteen years earlier, missionaries had arrived with the intention of converting the Hawaiians, who believed in many gods, into Christians.

Liliu was born at an important time in Hawaiian history. Great Britain and the United States were turning their attention to the islands and planning to take control of them. The missionaries were beginning to make progress in converting Hawaiians. And sugar was becoming an important and lucrative export, which led to foreigners running sugar plantations there.

Like many of the royal children, Liliu was given a Christian name, and she was known as Lydia as a child. At the age of four, she was sent to the Chiefs' Children's School, a boarding school for the royal children and the children of high chiefs. There, she learned to read and write in English. In her first year at the school,

1843, Hawaii fell under British rule. Although on July 31 of the same year Hawaiian independence was restored, the kingdom's fragility became even more pronounced. For the next four years, Restoration Day was celebrated with much fanfare. But then, in 1848, more changes came to Hawaii.

Although Hawaiian royalty still sat on the throne, Hawaii was now controlled by missionaries and foreign businessmen. The language, the money, the newspaper, the teachers, and the business owners were all becoming increasingly American. Liliu, like many of the princes, became anti-American and was strongly opposed to the annexation of Hawaii to America. Although some of the royal princes leaned toward British rule, Liliu wanted a Hawaii for Hawaiians. However, after Kamehameha III died in 1854, Prince Liholiho was named Kamehameha IV, and he favored British control of Hawaii.

Liliu began to see the plight of her people. In an effort to battle the diseases that were killing so many native Hawaiians, she went door-to-door raising money to build a hospital in Honolulu. In addition, she became an active member of the Kaahumanu Society, an organization made up of high chiefesses who wanted to preserve Hawaiian traditions and culture as well as fortify the strength of its women, who were losing more and more power in a British-influenced government.

In 1862, Liliu married John Dominis, the son of an Italian sea captain. They had met briefly while attending the Chiefs' Children's School, then remet years later. The marriage proved to be an unhappy one, mainly due to the clash of the two cultures. Liliu's husband and mother-in-law criticized her English, her handwriting, and even her Hawaiian love of nature and flowers. Her unhappiness led her to spend much of her time traveling to the other Hawaiian islands.

Kamehameha IV died at the age of twenty-nine, a year after Liliu married. Hawaiians believed that he had died because he could not bear to live in a *haole*, or foreigner's, world. Prince Lot proclaimed himself king, and took the throne as Kamehameha V. Aware that the cultures were clashing, he drew up a new constitution in 1864 that gave him and his cabinet greater power. It was said of Kamehameha V that after he became king, he became more Hawaiian by the day.

The same can be said of Liliu. Her husband had been named governor of Oahu in 1868, and in her new role as first lady, she had witnessed again and again the loss of Hawaiian culture. When Kamehameha V decided to replace the British anthem "God Save the Queen" with a new Hawaiian national anthem, he asked Liliu to write it. That song is still the unofficial Hawaiian national anthem today.

When Kamehameha V died in 1872 without naming a successor, Prince Lunalilo was elected king. He promised to restore the old constitution of 1852, which favored the *haole*, or foreigners. After reigning for only a year, he died, and Liliu's brother, David Kalākaua, became the next king, which made her Princess Liliuokalani. In addition, he named her heir to the throne. When he died in 1891, she became Queen Liliuokalani. By this time, her Hawaii had changed even more. More and more Americans had moved to Hawaii, and the movement to make Hawaii a United States territory was strong. In 1893, the queen was removed from the throne. Still, she tried to gain a new constitution that would benefit her people. When she failed through the legislative process, she attempted to do so through a monarchal edict.

Liliuokalani was arrested on January 16, 1895, several days after a failed revolution. At her trial she denied knowledge of firearms that had been found at Diamond Head Crater, but she was still sentenced to five years of hard labor in prison by a military tribunal and fined five thousand dollars. Ultimately, the sentence was commuted to imprisonment in an upstairs bedroom of her home in the palace. To the horror and indignation of the Hawaiian people, Liliuokalani was a prisoner in her own home for almost two years. She was forbidden to leave the palace and was under constant watch. There she composed songs, including "The Queen's Prayer" and "Aloha 'Oe," which many believed was her farewell song to her beloved country. It is still a treasured and popular love song in Hawaii.

She was freed on October 6, 1896, and for the rest of her life Liliuokalani fought against the annexation of Hawaii to the United States, and watched as American interests took over the government, the businesses, and even the population of Hawaii. She wrote a book, *Hawaii's Story by Hawaii's Queen*. In late October 1917, little red fish appeared in the waters around Hawaii. According to Hawaiian beliefs, this predicted the death of an *ali'i*. On November 11, Liliuokalani, the last queen of Hawaii, died. At her request, in her casket she wore the crown that she had been forbidden to wear in her later years. On August 21, 1959, Hawaii became the fiftieth state of the United States.

Herman Melville

August 1, 1819–September 28, 1891

Herman Melville was born in New York City on August 1, 1819. When he was twenty-one years old, he left Fairhaven, Massachusetts, on a whaling ship to the Pacific Ocean. Melville often said that was the day his life really began. In 1842, while in the Marquesas Islands, he jumped ship and lived for three weeks with a tribe of cannibals called the Typee. From there, he sailed on an Australian whaler bound for Tahiti and spent several months as an *omoo*—Tahitian for "island rover." He then signed on to another whaler heading for Honolulu, where he worked setting pins in a bowling alley before becoming a store clerk. Melville was a controversial figure in Honolulu because of his opposition to the Christian missionaries and their treatment of native Hawaiians. After several months in Honolulu, he returned to Boston on a frigate.

His experiences in the Pacific are described in his novels *Typee*, *Omoo*, and *Moby-Dick*, the last of which was published in 1851. Although he gained some early literary success, when he died in 1891 he was broke, and he and his books were mostly forgotten. Decades after his death, his work once again found an audience. Herman Melville's *Moby-Dick* is now considered one of the greatest literary masterpieces of all time.

I do so much research for each book in the Treasure Chest series and discover so many cool facts that I can't fit into every book. Here are some of my favorites from my research for *The Treasure Chest: #6 Queen Liliuokalani: Royal Prisoner.* Enjoy!

Fun facts about 1959

On August 21, 1959, Hawaii became the fiftieth state. Earlier that year, on January 3, Alaska became the forty-ninth state. No new states have been admitted since Hawaii.

The president was Dwight D. Eisenhower.

Fidel Castro took over Cuba.

American Airlines flew the first transcontinental commercial jet trip from Los Angeles to New York. A round-trip ticket cost about $238. What we now call John F. Kennedy Airport, or JFK, in New York City was then called Idlewild.

The first Grammys were awarded in 1959. The winners included Ella Fitzgerald and Perry Como.

Three of the top new television shows that fall were *Bonanza*, *The Twilight Zone*, and *The Many Lives of Dobie Gillis*. *Bonanza* ran for fourteen years, *The Twilight Zone* ran for five, and *The Many Loves of Dobie Gillis* ran for four. One of the stars of *Dobie Gillis* was Bob Denver, who played the beatnik Maynard G. Krebs. From 1964 to 1967, Denver played Gilligan on *Gilligan's Island*.

Walt Disney released the animated movie *Sleeping Beauty* in 1959.

On November 16, 1959, *The Sound of Music* opened on Broadway. It played for 1,443 performances and won the Tony Award for Best Musical. Although Julie Andrews starred in the 1965 film version, Mary Martin played the role of Maria von Trapp on Broadway and won the Tony Award for Best Actress in a Musical.

The story of *The Sound of Music* is based on that of a real family. The von Trapps lived in a villa outside

Salzburg, Austria. In 1926, Maria was sent to work as a tutor for one of the von Trapp children, who was recovering from scarlet fever. Unlike the fictional von Trapps, who had seven children, the real von Trapps had ten. The play and the film changed the names and the ages of the children, and had Maria become the governess to all of them. They also presented the character of Colonel von Trapp, the children's father, as a cold, distant man. But the real Colonel von Trapp loved music and was known to be kind and warmhearted. The family did not escape across the Alps after a musical contest. Instead, they left by train to Italy and then continued on to London. They ultimately came to the United States, settling in Vermont, where the mountains reminded them of their home in Austria. In the summer of 1950, the family opened the Trapp Family Lodge in Stowe, Vermont, which is still operated by the von Trapps today. Four of the ten von Trapp children are still alive.

Also, in 1959, Barbie made her debut. Prior to Barbie, dolls were almost always baby dolls. But a woman named Ruth Handler noticed that when her daughter Barbara played with her dolls, she always pretended they were adults. Ruth Handler's husband was cofounder of the Mattel toy company, and she presented her idea of a doll that looked like a grown-up to him. He told her it was a bad idea.

Traveling in Germany, Ruth Handler saw a doll called Bild Lilli, based on a popular German comic strip. The doll looked like an adult. She was blond and had many outfits. Handler brought one home with her and eventually convinced her husband and Mattel to make an American doll like it.

The first Barbie wore a black-and-white zebra-striped one-piece bathing suit. She featured either a blond or brunette ponytail.

The designer Charlotte Johnson designed her wardrobe. All the clothes were made in Japan, hand-stitched by Japanese women in their homes.

In her first year, three hundred thousand Barbies were sold.

Ann Hood, the author of the Treasure Chest series, owned one of those first Barbies! Hers was blond.

Today, over a billion Barbies have been sold worldwide.

Three Barbies are sold every second.

1959 was also a big year in baseball.

The New York Yankees had dominated baseball throughout the 1950s, appearing in eight out of ten World Series.

At the beginning of the decade, there were three New York baseball teams: the Yankees, the Giants, and the Brooklyn Dodgers. But in the 1950s, many baseball teams moved. The Boston Braves went to Milwaukee in 1953; the St. Louis Browns went to Baltimore in 1954, becoming the Baltimore Orioles; the Philadelphia Athletics went to Kansas City in 1955; and then, in 1958, the New York Giants moved to San Francisco, and the Brooklyn Dodgers moved to Los Angeles, leaving only the Yankees in New York until the Mets arrived in 1962.

The Brooklyn Dodgers had won four out of the last six National League pennants before they arrived in LA. But in their debut season there, they finished two games out of last place. However, in 1959 they made it to the World Series against the Chicago White Sox.

The White Sox had not made a postseason appearance since 1919, when the team threw the World Series, intentionally losing games so that the Cincinnati

Reds would win the series. Known as the Black Sox, eight players from that team, including their star outfielder, "Shoeless" Joe Jackson, were banned from Major League Baseball for life.

The LA Dodgers won the series against the White Sox, four games to two. The White Sox did not make another World Series appearance until 2005, when they swept the Houston Astros. But the LA Dodgers went on to win four more World Series, in 1963, 1965, 1981, and 1988.

**Continue your adventures in
The Treasure Chest!**

THE TIME-TRAVELING ADVENTURES OF THE ROBBINS TWINS
THE TREASURE CHEST
ALEXANDER GRAHAM BELL: MASTER OF SOUND
BY NEW YORK TIMES BEST-SELLING AUTHOR
ANN HOOD

THE TREASURE CHEST

DON'T MISS ANY OF THESE ADVENTURES!

www.treasurechestseries.com